I0547283

pine for you

pine for you

A HOLIDAY ROMANTIC SUSPENSE NOVELLA

PINESBURY, REIMAGINED

J.M. LEIGH

ALEXIS LAYNE

Pine for You

By: J.M. Leigh and Alexis Layne

Published By: Happileigh Ever After, LLC

Copyright © 2023 Happileigh Ever After, LLC & Alexis Layne

This book is an original publication of J.M. Leigh and Alexis Layne. All rights reserved.

This book is a work of fiction. All names, characters, places, and events are fictional or used fictitiously. Any resemblance is coincidental. No part of this book may be reproduced, scanned, or distributed in any form without prior written permission from the copyright owner, with the exception of brief quotations used for book review purposes.

To request permission, contact authorjmleigh@gmail.com.

Paperback: 979-8-9872569-5-4

Ebook: 979-8-9872569-4-7

First edition: December 8th, 2023

www.jmleigh.com

❀ Created with Vellum

To all of those learning to love Christmas again.

pine for you

Rosie Atwood is overwhelmed. Christmas used to be her favorite time of year, but everything changed five years ago when her best friend ghosted her right before she could tell him how she really felt. And it's all gone downhill since. When her sister dies, and Rosie's left in charge of her young nephew, she's willing to do whatever she needs to protect him from the Atwood curse. Including becoming a surrogate for her oldest sister in exchange for meals and a place to live. Her last dream is to turn things around for Waldvogel Farms. Holden's grandparents are the best family she ever had, and she refuses to let them down. But being pregnant and thrust into the role of parent doesn't make it easy. Then Holden Moore shows back up, ready to reclaim his spot in her life like nothing changed. Rosie thinks things can't get any worse. Until someone starts sabotaging all the work she'd done to save the Farm. Is Holden behind the damage? Using it as an excuse to get close to her? Or is there something more sinister at play?

Holden Moore never intended to leave Pinesbury behind. He just wanted to be a soldier. And he wanted to be the kind of man his best friend could love. But a close call on his first deployment made Holden reevaluate everything he'd ever known. Afraid he wouldn't be there for Rosie or his family back home, Holden cut ties. Now he's back in town, five years later, and ready to leave combat behind and right his wrongs. It's just too bad Rosie isn't ready to welcome him back into her life. But Holden is determined to change her mind. When things start going wrong at Waldvogel Farms, Holden finds himself blamed by the town that helped raise him. Juggling the hunt for the mysterious saboteur, rebuilding his relationship with Rosie, and fighting his status as Pinesbury's Fallen Golden Boy wasn't how he planned to spend his first Christmas back, but when an innocent gets caught in the middle, Holden has no choice but to tap into his old training or risk losing everything.

With Happily Ever After on the line, will Rosie and Holden be able to heal old wounds and save Waldvogel Farms in time for Christmas? Or will it all go down in flames?

Stay up to date on the latest releases, get sneak peeks, and exclusive bonus content by subscribing to the Escape Reality newsletter.

reader notes

This book is told in dual, alternating POV. All odd chapters are in Rosie's POV, and all even chapters are in Holden's POV. The prologue and epilogue are told in the POV of both characters and a subheading is used to indicate the speaker.

TRIGGERS

This book contains adult content and content referencing adult situations, the loss of a sibling/parent, emotional neglect, abduction of a child, infertility, and trauma, including on-page discussions of violence. While our goal in writing this story was to provide entertainment and escape and situations and experiences have been simplified to that end, these topics are heavy and deserving of care and understanding.

If you live in the US and need to talk, dial 988 for the Suicide and Crisis Lifeline.

"Christmas, my child, is love in action. Every time we love, every time we give, it's Christmas." - Dale Evans

the last letter

ROSIE

I'D BEEN HOME for three days, but it didn't feel like it until I stepped foot on Waldvogel Farms. The whispering winter winds that chilled my nose and the woody crunch of bark and snow underfoot provided a sense of calm I couldn't get anywhere close to at my house. Even with all three of us all grown up, my sisters and I still congregated there. And that meant someone was always yelling about something.

I would have escaped to the Farm sooner if my parents and sisters hadn't monopolized all my time helping them navigate their latest drama. Why it was the responsibility of the youngest member of the family to keep the peace, I'd never know. The arguments had only gotten worse since I'd gone to school in Connecticut. Two states away from Vermont for my own sanity, but close enough to make coming home easy. Unfortunately, *only-two-states-away* was still enough for the feud between my sisters to reach a whole new level.

I forced back the intrusive thoughts and focused on taking in everything on the walk through my favorite place in the world. My destination was just up ahead, hidden amongst a small patch of trees, the quaint little house covered in Germanic influences and the start of this season's Christmas decor, a cloud of smoke puffing determinedly into the sky from the stone chimney. The only signs of life this early on a winter morning.

A rush of warmth enveloped me as I opened the door. I took a deep breath, inhaling aromas of cinnamon and sugar and oranges deep into my chest, before beginning the process of un-layering, and called out for Oma.

"*Röschen*, I thought we would never see you," Holden's grandmother hollered back from the kitchen, "Opa is in the barn looking for decorations."

I walked through to find her tapping her hands on her once-red apron. Now it had taken on a shade of pink, it was so covered in flour. But that explained the smell.

She wrapped me up in a hug that left me covered in flour, too. Then *tsk*-ed and laughed at herself as she dusted at my clothes. "Your apron is in the pantry, *Röschen*, it is not safe for clothes without it. Go get it, come help with the cookies."

Hours later, my hands ached from rolling dough and my belly was stuffed full of the first batch of seasonal treats. Oma and I settled ourselves at the table overlooking the back of the farm. We talked about everything as we worked. How school was going, what I'd learned this semester, my family, and their never-ending drama. But the conversation always came back around to the only child of her only child.

"I like him, Oma," I admitted quietly, "I always have. But he has enough on his mind, enough to worry about over there."

"I know, my dear," she patted my hand a little firmly on the rough kitchen table, "But these things, you cannot wait forever." Then she huffed, "And you cannot rely on men to speak first. They are scared like children when it comes to love. My Otto would have waited six more years if I had not told him to take me out."

I sighed and pulled my hand back, wrapping it tightly around the mug, hoping it might warm up just a little courage. "I know. Next time I write to him, I'll tell him we need to talk. Maybe we can manage a video call."

I was already thinking about the letter sitting at home. We'd been talking about school, and Christmas, and how my sisters' feud had been getting even more out of control. The same things I talked about with his grandmother, the same things I couldn't talk about with anyone who wasn't of Waldvogel descent.

Oma hummed, not quite satisfied with my compromise, but not pushing me any harder either.

Holden –

I'm back from school for the winter and the Farm is doing great. This year's decorations might be almost as good as last year's. But it's always better when you're there helping out. It's just not Christmas here without you. Opa Waldvogel needs help sometimes and you're way better at the fixing up stuff than I am, but I'm trying my best. He insisted on climbing the ladder to put the star up since you weren't here. He wouldn't even think of letting me do it. Oma wasn't happy either, we both hope you'll be here next year.

You know how my sisters are. They literally won't stop arguing, even though they've been adults long enough to know better. I'm afraid if they can't figure it out, they'll lose each other completely. And I'll be stuck in the middle. I know that's a selfish thing to worry about, but I can't help it. I love them both. I guess I'm just scared they'll ask me to choose.

I talked to Oma. You know how great of a listener she is. She always helps me feel better. I hope you're taking the time to write them letters, too. They miss you. I miss you. Call me when you get a chance, there's something important I need to talk to you about.

Please be safe.

Always,
Rosie

It took another two weeks after Oma and I talked to get the courage to finish the letter. I dropped it off on the way to the farm. I hoped it wouldn't take weeks to hear back this time. I wasn't sure how much longer I could wait to tell him how I felt. And I hoped even more that telling him wouldn't be a mistake.

Because I didn't think I could live without Holden Moore in my life, even if that meant we'd only get to be friends.

HOLDEN

Nine months ago, I was having nightmares about pre-calc tests that I'd already taken and passed. Now, my dreams were filled with the sounds of gunfire and exploding IEDs. Sometimes, I woke up to the real thing.

The *whomp, whomp, whomp* of helicopter blades cutting through the thick, sandy air filled my ears as I braced myself against the bench. The radios had gone silent, all of us too deep in our own thoughts. Lost to repeating the facts of the mission, or desperately trying to avoid them.

I'd already replayed the briefing in my mind a thousand times, and I hadn't gotten any less scared as shit. I wasn't too tough to admit it to myself, but I'd be damned if I said it out loud. I hoped no one else would, either. That'd just be asking for trouble. There wasn't much difference between the theater and the theater of war. Both were damn superstitious.

But I couldn't be stuck in my mind over it anymore, either. I pulled the latest letter from Rosie out of my pocket instead, carefully unfolding it and tracing a hand over the messy, feminine script. I'd reread it more times than I'd replayed the brief, but that didn't matter. I could read it a million times and not get enough. The rest of her letters were kept neatly tucked away in my footlocker. Stored more reverently than anything else I had in this damn desert.

I wasn't the only one, either. All around me, new brothers were opening their own letters from home. Reminding ourselves why we were here, why we did what we did. Making sure their words were right there at the front of our minds, knowing they might be the last we ever got to read.

I pulled out a pen and my all-weather notebook from another pocket and braced it against my knee to finally write back.

Rosie –

Don't let him get it down!!! Opa is too damn stubborn. My dad will help, I'll make sure he finds a reason to be there when it's time to take the decorations down. I really wish I could be there to see them, send me pictures.

"Fuck, I don't know about this one," Henson murmured as I punctuated the end of my sentence. I grit my teeth. *So much for not saying that shit out loud.*

"Dude, shut the fuck up," Frazier spat back, cutting off any further foreboding. I nodded silently, then turned back to my notebook.

I hope they figure it out. You're all each other have. If there's anything I've learned out here, it's that you don't know how many days you have left.

Static in my ears interrupted the reply I was working on this time. I ripped the page from my notebook and folded my letter up in Rosie's, then shoved them both in my chest pocket. Right over my heart. My good luck charm. If the intel was right, we were going to need it.

I woke up two days later at a makeshift hospital on a FOB way back from enemy lines. Hours away from the location of my last dark memories. The thick smell of gunpowder and metallic blood infiltrated my mind, but I forced it, and the memories, back.

It took every bit of energy I had to push myself up and look around. A dull pain in my abdomen cued me into the reason I was here. Another flashback pushed its way into my brain. Looking down at my shattered vest, blood on my hands, gripping the textbook-sized shrapnel tucked jaggedly into my abdomen.

I blinked away the picture again. Focused on the barely sterile room. I was alone, for now. Sounds of voices and boots stomping suggested it wouldn't be long. Crates stacked next to me made up a side table and I leaned over when I caught a glimpse of folded notebook paper under a stack of other shit I couldn't care less about right then.

It hurt to reach out and grab them, but not as much as I expected it would based on my last memories and the initial pain I'd woken up to. Blood had seeped into both sheets of paper. I read Rosie's letter first, her familiar handwriting carried me thousands of miles away. Back to the tiny town of Pinesbury, Vermont. Then the sounds of yelled voices roughly dragged me back to the desert, chilling my blood despite the stifling heat. I pulled the response I'd been working on back out.

The last words I wrote stared back at me. It was true, but maybe too true. I couldn't remember many of the fine details yet, but one thing was sure: I shouldn't even be alive to see these letters. The stitches I felt tugging at my abdomen were evidence of that. And the only reason why I'd still be in the desert instead of some only slightly more serviceable hospital in Germany is because they expected me back in the field before long.

I wracked my addled brain trying to think of what Rosie could want to talk about. Whatever it was, she couldn't put it in a letter, and she spilled her heart out in those things. Sometimes I'd get envelopes that were six pages thick. This one was barely a page, so it was too big for anything else to be on her mind.

I folded up her letter and looked back down at mine. My heart pounded in my chest. I'd been half in love with Rosie Atwood since Kindergarten. What if she met someone? I wasn't sure I could handle it. *But what if she didn't?* And that was even worse. Because I wasn't fucking sure I'd be alive for it.

Fear made me tear up my letter. I never sent one back.

FIVE YEARS LATER.

"Ri, let's go, buddy," I called with desperate patience. Not for the first time, I found myself blinking back tears. I shoved my sunglasses down over my face so Orion wouldn't see them as he toddled down the stairs. I still wanted to curse my sister, I really did. But I understood why Daisy did it. Still, I wasn't ready. Even nine months in. I wasn't even sure being a mom was in the cards for me anymore.

I tried to move on, but no one could compete with the memory of Holden Moore. But unlike my sister, Holden was only dead to me.

"Bay-be," Orion stopped a couple of steps from the bottom and rubbed his hands over my stomach. I was officially showing now and it was just another weird, unbelievable part of my life. Two kids that weren't even mine, and I was entirely responsible for keeping both alive right now. I'd be responsible for Orion for the rest of his life, though, and that sent another rush of tears to my eyes. *Damn pregnancy hormones.*

I pressed my palms over his tiny hands, "That'll be your

little cousin, Ri. We're keeping Auntie Lily's baby safe for her, aren't we?"

"Cuh-zin. Safe," the two-and-a-half-year-old tested the syllables. Their age difference would be about the same as my sisters. And I found myself praying Daisy's and Lily's kids got along better than they did.

"Time to get your jacket on, kiddo," I squeezed his hands under mine, and it was the exact wrong thing to say.

"No!" He screamed in his tiny, but *very* highly-pitched voice, then turned around and dashed back up the stairs. "No. Jack-ett," he was still screaming as he disappeared down the hallway.

This time I didn't even try to stop the tears from falling.

We were an hour late to the farm, and even though I knew they wouldn't hold it against me, I was struggling to swallow the guilt. Oma and Opa loved me like I was their own, but seeing them all the time hurt. I managed when I was just coming back to visit. I could fake it for a week or two. But I moved back after Daisy died. Her last wish. Because she didn't trust our sister or parents to care for Orion, and I couldn't bear to tear him away from the little family he had left. So, now, every day was a reminder. Every day hurt.

"Oh-ma!" Daisy's spitting image squealed, his arms flinging toward the loving, and oh-so-painful reminder, nearly sending me toppling over as I pulled him from the car seat.

"Careful, little star," she tutted, pulling him from my arms.

"Star, star," he chanted as I tugged his diaper bag from the floor of the backseat. I almost sent myself over again when the strap got caught on a box of Christmas decorations the Waldvo-gels had given me to decorate Orion's and my room two weeks ago. I still hadn't taken them out. I didn't think I even liked Christmas anymore.

Oma took the bag with a shake of her head, then slung it over her shoulder. "Röschen," she murmured quietly, tapping my cheek with her free hand. The touch weighed heavily with words unspoken.

"Ro-, raw-," Orion frowned, attempting the German sounds. A sob worked its way up my throat, burning deeply, and I coughed to cover it up. I wouldn't be able to handle it if the little boy started calling me that, too. It was bad enough that Oma still did, but I didn't have the heart to ask her to stop. To tell her that it reminded me too much of her grandson.

Mercifully, Oma left me to collect myself, toting Orion along with her with promises of cookies and a ride in the red truck Opa used to deliver trees. I tipped my head against the SUV's doorframe. My shoulders wracked a few times, but I managed to keep the actual tears back. Thankfully. I hadn't felt like fixing my mascara twice in two hours. Maybe I should just stop wearing it. It would save me five bucks the next time I went to the store, and every penny counted when I was literally counting pennies.

Taking a deep breath, I stepped back and slammed the door. Just a little rougher than I needed to because it made me feel better. Then I grabbed my bag from the front passenger seat and slammed that door, too, before turning to walk up the path that used to bring me so much solace.

I'd hoped to get in early to work on the business loan proposal I'd started four months ago. Waldvogel Farms needed help. Opa, Oma, and I did our best, but they were getting old, and no matter how hard I tried, I was never as handy as Holden had been. We needed money for repairs, and then we needed to expand. It was the only way to keep the farm running, to keep it from getting run out by the larger commercial tree vendors that popped up in parking lots and dormant fields in the bigger towns nearby.

Because of their scale, they could out-price us. And they did. So the farm had been bringing in less and less, falling deeper and deeper into disrepair. But I had a plan. We just needed to find our feet again. Then I wanted to open up during all seasons. Offer corn mazes in the fall, host community events and weddings year-round. But between being pregnant, going to doctor's appointments, and caring for a grieving child, I hadn't had the time and energy I needed to complete the proposal.

The ice on the path I walked felt like the slippery slope we were on. If I didn't finish it soon, we wouldn't have enough to show for the loan. No big ideas, no matter how good, could convince a bank to give us more money when we couldn't pay the bills we had. The way I saw it, this season was our last chance. If we could just do a little better than break even this year, my proposal would have some legs to stand on.

But, because of a stupid jacket, we were late. And the chores on the farm weren't going to do themselves. With only another hour before we opened, I sighed and headed to the little cottage that served as a small office. If we weren't busy after opening, I could work on the proposal. But if we weren't busy after opening, the proposal would be a waste of time.

I couldn't win.

We weren't *busy* after opening, but the place wasn't dead either. The work kept me too occupied to do anything on the proposal, but traffic was steady enough to make breaking even possible. As long as it kept up for the rest of the season.

My feet ached from standing at the window where we

checked out customers all day. Opa had brought in a stool for me last week, but it wasn't quite tall enough. And standing up and sitting down over and over hurt more than just standing.

The flow of customers was slowing down with only thirty minutes left until closing. I was grateful I'd finally get to rest, and then I felt guilty because I didn't have time to rest. Not without sacrificing something I was unwilling to give up. Like dinner with Orion and the Waldvogels, and a couple hours to work on the proposal before I needed to get him home to sleep.

"Rosie!" The last customer in line practically cheered my name. I looked up from the delivery notes I'd been writing and squinted at the man.

"Hello," I smiled, somewhat awkwardly. He looked maybe a little familiar, and he definitely knew who I was. But I couldn't place him. I hoped he didn't notice.

He did. "It's me! Conrad Clarke, don't you remember? It hasn't been that long!" He held his arms out wide, as if expecting me to hug him through the wall.

It took a minute, but when the name finally registered, I nodded. I attempted another smile, too, but I was just so tired. Catching up with someone from high school was the last thing I wanted right now. Everyone had expected so much from me, had expected Holden and I to end up together, like some sort of sweet Hallmark story.

It was bad enough that everyone in our small town knew that hadn't happened, but at least I was always too busy to stop and chat with the ones who hadn't left yet. To witness the pity and disappointment on their faces. Until today.

A shrieking sound startled me, but I was almost grateful for the distraction. Until Orion came running from a patch of trees, horror on his face and his hands shoved out in front of him. Panic overwhelmed me and I stepped from the cottage in a hurry to meet him. I felt Conrad only a few paces behind.

When Orion caught up to me, he was still shrieking and doing absolutely nothing to explain what was wrong. My stomach lurched. Helplessness overwhelmed. *I can't do this. I can't be a parent.*

"Whoa, buddy, what's wrong?" Conrad spoke over my shoulder. It wasn't necessarily endearing, but not everyone was good around kids. I sure wasn't, even if I thought I had been. At least he was trying.

The new voice was at least enough to distract my nephew, who stopped shrieking and stared up at the man hovering above us, before returning his focus to me, crouched precariously in front of him. My muscles groaning their displeasure.

"Off!" He screamed and shoved his hands in my face. Not an answer, but a clue. I gripped his wrists gently and examined his palms. They were sticky with sap, like he'd been playing in the trees. It wasn't unusual, and he didn't like it, but it didn't usually set him off like this.

I twisted his hands gently and then noticed it. Half of a little insect, very dead, and stuck securely to the sap on his little finger. I looked at his other hand again and found the other half on his index finger. He'd obviously tried to pick it off, then tore it apart, and it just kept sticking. "C'mon," I murmured, readying myself to stand and walk him inside to clean it off.

"I think I can help," Conrad spoke up again from over my shoulder. I glanced back to see him tapping his pockets, checking inside a few, before he came out with a paper napkin. He finally crouched down next to me and plucked the bug parts from Orion's hands. Orion frowned, but let him. "Daisy's kid, right?"

I nodded wearily. That Daisy had died and left me in charge wasn't a secret in town, either. But Lily wasn't the only one who had a problem with Daisy—or the rest of my family—so where some small-town support might have been expected, none was found. I was supposed to be the exception to the Atwood scourge. Until I wasn't.

"Baby oil," he said, standing and offering a palm out to me. I took it, grateful for a little support, but frowning in confusion, "It helps get the sap off."

I nodded again. My mind finally catching up. Oma used mayonnaise, but the reasoning tracked. And I couldn't stand the smell of mayo now, so I was actually pretty happy to have an alternative. My smile must have shown it because Conrad grinned back.

"Maybe this is a bad time," he started, after I'd settled Orion on my hip. Conrad passed him more napkins as he spoke, and Ri gripped them in both hands, then stared in amusement as they stuck to and shredded apart from the sap. "But I'd love to buy you dinner. Catch up."

I sighed. It wasn't a great time. And as nice as Conrad had been, he wasn't Holden. But I forced a smile, because, after five years of radio silence, there was no way *that* Christmas wish would ever come true. And I was pretty sure Conrad had had a crush on me throughout high school. But, like everyone else, he would have thought Holden and I would progress to more-than-friends eventually. Then we didn't.

"No pressure, I know you're busy," he spoke again when I didn't. "And this little guy can come, too," he gestured awkwardly to the child in my arms.

"Orion," I finally said something. Not an answer, but it felt weird that he was inviting Ri without knowing his name. I sighed. I needed to move on. Or at least pretend I was willing to. "Maybe after the holidays? There's just too much going on right now."

Conrad bristled a little, but nodded. Then he leaned forward to kiss my cheek. I froze, totally thrown by the intimate gesture. "Good seeing you, Rosie," he said, still too close to my face. He finally stepped back and shoved his hands in his pockets, nodding once more to Orion before walking back down the path.

I turned and watched, Orion and I both staring after him, before I realized something—he never finished ordering his tree. *Dammit.*

I wasn't sure what to expect coming home. But it wasn't a dozen *For Sale* signs and half of Main Street closed up. I guessed I shouldn't have been surprised. My own parents had left Pinesbury. But they weren't the sentimental type. Still, all the faces I saw were familiar. A few stopped on the sidewalk and stared, spinning to continue watching as the car drove by.

At first, I thought nothing had changed. Despite my parent's brief comments telling me otherwise. As we rolled into town, Rowe's Tavern, the bar that had been home to my first fight, and just about every other Pinesbury male's, was still there. The old sign had dilapidated even more, and now the light from the *T* had gone out, too, joining the *O* and *V* that had been out for as long as I could remember. But it had been flickering for years so it wasn't that unexpected.

It was everything else that had me shaken up. The park was deserted, the playground half roped off where the monkey bars had broken away and were hanging dangerously. The diner that we'd always ditch school to have lunch at was closed. Some formal-looking paper tacked up to the window suggesting the reason was something more than just lack of business.

"*This* is home?" Frazier commented from the driver's seat. It wasn't really a question. He was making note of the fact that my little hometown looked nothing like how I'd described it these last five years. Pinesbury wasn't perfect, but I'd always remembered it as a quaint little Vermont town. The kind they had on the Hallmark shows Rosie liked to watch.

"I don't know what happened," I murmured, catching the eye of old Mrs. Danforth. She scowled back at me until the car was too far to sustain contact. At least something hadn't changed. She still hated me for breaking her window with a baseball thirteen years ago.

I felt Frazier glance over at me. "Creepy," he muttered. I found myself nodding. While there were a few Christmas decorations strung up on the businesses still open, mainly the library, the whole town was giving more Halloween than Hallmark. Especially as the light faded around us.

At the end of the street, he turned and I sat forward again to see the Pinesbury Inn coming into view. Somehow, I'd always remembered it being more stately. A landmark. The kind of place people would have posted about on social media and flocked to in droves during the high seasons. Now, the white painted trim had a gray cast. Several of the flower boxes that the Pickerings had always kept rotated with seasonal foliage had broken off, leaving the Federal-style façade unbalanced in a disconcerting way.

Frazier pulled up in front of the building and pressed hard on the break instead of putting the car in park, "You sure you want me to leave you here?"

I let my eyes widen uncertainly for a second, then nodded. "Yep. For now." I didn't have a reservation, and I'd been worried I'd have to sleep in the barn at the Farm, but this place felt deserted.

"Alright, man," he said hesitantly, throwing his 'retirement' gift into *Park* and popping the trunk. Frazier's yellow Mustang was the most vibrant thing in this town now. "Call me when you're ready to run."

I grinned back and shook my head. After I tugged my duffle from his trunk, I slammed it shut and tapped the hood. Frazier took off without a glance back.

I took a steadying breath, then climbed the steps. Up close, I could see a few things less broken down. It looked like a new door had been installed, the windows on either side had been scrubbed clean, and some of the exterior millwork had been replaced. A small bell rang when I pushed the door open and a guy a bit older than me stepped out from one of the side rooms.

"Hey, looking for a room?" He was wiping something off his hands with a dirty work rag.

I nodded, "Yeah, if you've got any."

He grinned like I just told a joke, "Got any? I got all of them. I'm not really open, but I can't be turning away business either. Hope you're good with the bare minimum."

My head bobbed slowly. I'd lived for years with less than what people back home considered the bare minimum, so that wasn't a problem. But something else was. "What happened to the Pickerings?" The family had been running the Inn for a hundred years. Maybe more. And this guy sure as shit wasn't a Pickering.

"Sold the place when their kids didn't want it," the man shrugged. "I ran it for a while as is, but it's just too far gone. Shut it down at the end of the summer, and I've been trying to restore it, but it's a hell of a project. The name's Eric, by the way."

"Holden," I took his outstretched hand. He seemed nice enough. I'd gotten pretty good at reading people over the years and this guy set off no red flags. But I was still unsettled. Nothing I remembered was the same. Well, except apparently the worst parts. Like grouchy Mrs. Danforth and the old bar that should have shut down twenty years ago. My heart sank at the thought that my favorite part of this whole damn town might be gone, too. Little Rosie Atwood. *Röschen.*

"You're from around here then?" I was still gripping Eric's hand and he was watching me with concern.

I tugged my palm back and blinked away the memories. "Yeah. Was, I guess. It wasn't like this when I left."

"Things started going downhill pretty quick about five years ago," he filled in a blank with an answer that sat like bad seafood in my stomach. I wasn't sure I could have made any difference, but guilt still left a sour taste.

I swallowed a lump in my throat and nodded.

"Well, take your pick of the rooms. I'd suggest something on the first floor, I'm having some water pressure issues," Eric tipped his head toward the old registration desk. It was covered in a beige painter's tarp, but behind it, the twelve room keys still hung in their pride of place. Then he turned and left like he hadn't just given free access to a complete stranger.

The floor creaked under me as I moved around the counter. I hesitated a moment, then grabbed the key to room number five. If I remembered correctly, it was tucked in the back corner on the opposite side of the building that Eric had come from. I slung my bag up a little higher on my shoulder and found my way back, dumping it on the unmade bed, and stepping into the en suite just as my phone started ringing.

"Holden!" Charlie Anderson's voice echoed into the empty bathroom. "Did you make it back okay?"

"I did," I answered tentatively. Frazier had already seen it, but I still felt reluctant to share the new reality of my hometown with my friends. Like it would somehow make it more real.

"Listen, I know you didn't leave things on the best footing. I just wanted you to know there's a spot on Bravo if you decide Pinesbury isn't for you." Charlie had a way of putting everyone at ease; and extracting all the things they didn't want to share. Which meant he was the only one in the world who knew the reality of my severed ties with this town. Who knew the guilt I carried over it.

"Thanks, man," I sighed, bracing myself on the bathroom counter. I had no desire to go back to the covert work I'd done in the Army, nor take up the security services Anderson Security offered as a cover, but I wasn't sure Pinesbury was going to be an option anymore, either. I hadn't been sure before, but seeing it now made me even more uncertain. "I'll think about it and get back to you."

"Sure, take as much time as you need," he hung up with a cheerful, "Merry Christmas!"

When it came to Pinesbury, I had no idea where to start. All I knew was that I needed to see Rosie. But first, I needed wheels. Dad had said the beat-up truck I drove around in high school was still in town. He was paying Old Man Metzger to keep it in his old auto garage. I didn't know if it was even still running, but there didn't seem to be many other options.

A cold breeze met me when I stepped out of the Inn. Eric had still been somewhere on the east side of the building if the loud hammering noise was any indication. I tried to think of who might still be around to hitch a ride from if the truck didn't turnover. Based on the *For Sale* signs, I was short on amicable neighbors. I wondered if Eric would be willing. But, luckily, a short walk was all it took to rule out the necessity of a Plan B.

I found Old Man Metzger fiddling with a Jeep that probably hadn't worked before I was born. *Guess he has time for old projects now*. I took in the faded garage. The sign was still there, but he'd been closing up shop when I was leaving. I found myself feeling grateful he hadn't sold it and left. But he was never a very sociable guy, so after a few words on my part, and a few grunts on his, I had the keys to my old, significantly dustier ride. The truck rattled as I pulled out of the parking lot and turned in the direction of Waldvogel Farms, just on the outskirts of town.

My mind wandered on the drive. It didn't take five years to realize what an idiot I'd been not writing back, but it had been long enough to make a letter seem insufficient. And every time I tried to go home or even just fucking call, something got in the way. Looking back, I'd been an idiot to give up at just that, too. I had made sure to always keep Oma updated. I could have tried harder. Should have tried harder.

Because now it was five years later and I hadn't said or written a damn word to Rosie in all that time. I prayed I wasn't too late. I pulled into the side entrance of the farm and killed the engine. The *tick, tick, tick* of the old truck filled the wintery silence. I couldn't tell if it was an ominous sound or not.

The smell of pine was entrancing walking into the farm, memories rushed in on me like a freight train. Flashbacks to a childhood spent running through lines of trees. The decorations hadn't changed much since the last Christmas I'd spent here. They looked a little older, but still evoked a wave of nostalgia that made me feel at home. *Finally.*

I picked up my pace, a little happier now. A little more encouraged. The infectious optimism of Christmas coursing through my veins, warming me up from the inside. I opted to take the long way around the farm, weaving through the trees, and coming up at the main entrance. My heart soared when I caught a glimpse of Rosie at the small window, taking care of a line of customers who'd brought up tickets for the trees they'd picked out. Five years had done nothing but good things, and even fifty yards away I could see her face glowing, a bright smile on her cold-pinkened lips.

And then my heart plummeted when a shrill scream had her running from the hut, the person at the window hustling after her. A little boy met her and was wailing as she frantically knelt in front of him. I watched as the man talked to the kid, which made him stop crying immediately. Rosie looked back at his hands. The man stooped down and helped with whatever was wrong. He helped her stand and she swooped up the kid to her hip, then he leaned forward and, from my angle, it sure looked like he was kissing her.

I ducked behind the old red truck Opa used for deliveries and had left parked at the front of the farm for some reason. I didn't know what I'd been thinking. Of course, she moved on. I ghosted her five years ago, but Rosie was too strong to let my betrayal weigh on her. She'd always had big dreams, and concrete plans to reach them. She was the only damn level head in the whole Atwood family.

When I stepped back around, the man with Rosie was gone and she was bouncing the little boy on her hip, whispering to him. I was stuck, I didn't know what to do. I didn't want to leave without seeing Oma and Opa at least. Especially not when I'd already left a message that morning saying I'd be there. But I wasn't sure I could face Rosie right then anymore. And to see them, I'd have to go through her.

And then it was too late. I witnessed the moment Rosie realized I was there. She looked up and I was close enough to see her face pale like she'd seen a ghost. I guessed that was pretty much what I was. I took a deep breath and forced myself to walk toward her.

"Rosie," I bit back the German nickname I'd wanted to use. It always came out a little more than friendly, not that I thought she ever picked up on it. Oma called her that, too. But I didn't think it was appropriate anymore. Not the way I said it.

"Holden," she breathed, more than said, my name. And fuck if I didn't feel it cut down to a place I hadn't let myself acknowledge for way too long. A million emotions I'd tucked into a neat little box, only trying to come out when I'd had too much to drink after a particularly bad op, exploded free from their confinement. I tried desperately to put them back, Rosie obviously didn't want them now.

"How are you?" I barely choked out the loaded question.

"I'm okay," she said slowly. Then the hand that wasn't being used to prop up the tiny human, who looked so much like her, came down to her belly and rubbed softly. It pressed back hard against her shirt and I realized she was pregnant. It hit me with so much force I felt my knees weaken, air punched out of my lungs.

"I, uh," I started, my eyes glued to her hand on the small, rounded bump. I didn't know what to say next. I shouldn't have come home at all. *Second biggest mistake you ever made, Moore.*

"Off," the little boy whimpered. Paper napkins were shredded and stuck to his hands and he stared down at them in distress.

"Sorry," we both said at the same time. Awkward tension vibrated in the cold air around us.

I couldn't fight the gulp. Or the need to run. "I'll, uh, I'll leave you to your son," I wanted to bite my own tongue off as I said the words.

A confused look flitted over her face, but then she nodded rapidly. "Yeah. My son," it even sounded funny when she said the word. "I have to go. Bye," she finished and spun on her heel, walking away with the fear and hurry of someone who'd been told their house was on fire.

I watched her leave. Pain squeezed my chest. Ice coated my lungs as I inhaled. I needed to see my grandparents. Then I planned on tucking tail and running away even faster than I did when I realized exactly where the ball was going to hit on Mrs. Danforth's house.

HOLDEN'S BACK. The thought just kept repeating in my mind the whole drive back to Lily's place. *Holden is in freaking Pinesbury.* Even the sight of his old truck parked not far from me felt like a painful stab to the chest. I was so... so gobsmacked... I didn't even care that Orion's sticky fingers were getting all over the backseat. It wasn't like it was that nice of a vehicle anyway. It ran. And it was safe for Ri. That was all I cared about.

Holden. My dumb, stupid, naive heart was thrilled about it. But it was too late for that Christmas wish to come true. Because Holden hadn't been trapped somewhere. *Oma always tells me when he's safe.*

He hadn't been forbidden from contact. *Oma says he calls twice a month.*

He hadn't even been too busy to keep up. *See above.*

He'd simply chosen to leave me and the rest of Pinesbury behind.

More tears burned in my eyes, and I wasn't even sure I could blame hormones for this one.

🌲

I guessed the one perk of Holden Moore throwing me so far off that I couldn't sleep was that, because I was awake, I was at least somewhat able to focus on some of the Waldvogel Farms projects I'd been working on. I glanced over my shoulder to the bed Orion and I shared. He was still sleeping peacefully. For now. I turned the brightness down on my laptop a little more, just in case.

Pinesbury wasn't the quaint little town it used to be. Many families had moved out, and the ones that stayed behind held onto the old grudges like they held on to their dilapidated properties—with zero interest in making anything better.

But a few of the nearby towns had started seeing new families move in. And, while some of them were falling victim to the mass commercialization of the cities not far away, some were rebuilding even sweeter than they had been before. In my research, I found that the towns that survived often had some feature or landmark that enticed people looking for those small-town vibes. Pinesbury didn't have that much anymore, but we could. Waldvogel Farms *was* a landmark, and it used to be quite the destination. Way back when.

Looking back, I realized that it had been slowing down for as long as I could remember. As kids, Holden and I could get up to just about anything on the Farms because it was never so busy that we'd upset customers. Unfortunately, that sweet childhood memory was evidence of the fact that Pinesbury and Waldvogel Farms had been losing their charm. But it didn't have to stay that way.

I'd already started by having Opa park the old truck at the front of the Farm. It needed a little work, too, but it was cute. It had character. And people wanted pictures with it. Pictures they would tag on social media and would help get the word out about the Farm. Tomorrow, I planned to drag an old bench over and a few decorations so the spot felt even more photogenic. And so it stayed photogenic and functional when Opa used the truck for deliveries.

I thought about what the old families would think of that. Of an Atwood reversing the downward spiral that Pinesbury had been on for the last two decades. There had already been some interest after I started the rather exhausting social media campaign before Daisy died. I hadn't really planned on coming back at the time, I just didn't want to see the Farm vanish like everyone else. I knew the old Inn had been bought up and I'd seen a few real estate agents showing off the empty storefronts on Main Street.

But then Daisy died and Lily asked for my help and I couldn't say no to either of their wishes. I tried to keep up the pace, but it was just too difficult alone. It was on my list to stop by the Inn and meet the new owner, but I hadn't found the time.

Orion stirred and whimpered on the bed behind me. I sighed, closing the laptop on the photo I'd been editing of him and Opa. Orion's face was obscured, but you could see the huge grin on Opa's as he held Orion up as high as he could while the toddler attempted to adorn the tree with a star. It was perfect, but the colors were flat. My degree was in business, not graphic design or photography. But I'd been trying to learn.

It would have to wait for another night, though, because I had less than two minutes to get him out of the nightmare before he screamed and woke up Lily. "Shh, buddy," I whispered, crawling back under the covers with him, tucking him up to my chest. Was two-and-a-half too young to see a therapist? *And how would I even afford it?*

I LOST sight of Rosie and her son behind the trees toward the side entrance where I'd parked. That meant that shitty SUV out there must have been hers. I felt anger swell up inside at the thought. Rosie wasn't a big car person, but she deserved more than that dented bucket of metal. Even if it ran okay, the paint was all chipped and it probably had terrible mileage and lumpy seats from decades of other people sitting on them.

Not that I had much room to talk, driving around my old truck. But that was only because I hadn't needed to buy a car in all the years I'd been gone. I was overseas more than I was home. There had been no point. A new one was on my list of things to take care of. And my old truck was *still* better than whatever she was driving. It may not have been driven much in the last five years, but I always took care of it. And it seemed like even Old Man Metzger had even taken on that responsibility. Rosie's husband was a sad sack of garbage for letting her drive their kids around in that.

I gritted my teeth and forced my steps toward Oma's house. *Not my problem.* The residence was tiny and tucked behind a copse of trees, hidden just enough from the main area of the

Farm and little office to offer some privacy, but close enough that Oma and Opa had always been able to comfortably split their days between caring for the Farm and caring for me, and then me and Rosie, at the house.

I hesitated at the thick wood door. Normally, I'd just walk right in. This was more home than the house I grew up in. But nothing felt right anymore, and I wasn't sure. Finally, I let my fist hit the door in a gentle knock before slowly pushing it open.

"Holden!" Oma rushed into the entryway with enthusiasm, my name sounding funny in her still-thick German accent. My parents were nice enough, but tradition wasn't their thing, and my mom, Oma's only child, had been undeniably Americanized.

"Oma," I let her tug me down to her short height so she could kiss my cheek and wrap me up in the kind of affectionate hug I hadn't experienced in half a decade.

"Look at you," she tapped my cheek then stepped back, "I did not think you could get taller, but I think maybe you did. Or maybe I got shorter. Come inside, have some cocoa. Opa will be back soon."

I followed her into the kitchen and settled at the familiar kitchen table. A flicker of twilight shone through the window, making the trees still barely visible, but shrouded in darkness. Everything was the same here, and I took a deep breath of relief.

"Was *Röschen* there? I thought she would have dinner with us tonight?" Oma asked, busying herself with a pot at the stove. Pouring a hot, rich concoction into two mugs. For a second, I felt myself salivating over the memory of her homemade cocoa, then I almost choked on my spit.

"Uh, yeah," I squeezed the edge of the table, desperate to do something to channel the intensity of what I was feeling somewhere other than my words, "She was in a hurry to take care of something with her son." My mind wandered to the guy I saw kissing her. If he was her husband, why hadn't he stayed to help? He left in the direction of the main parking lot, but Rosie went to the side lot.

"The baby is not hers," the stout old woman turned on me, her tone scolding. "Orion belonged to Daisy, but now Daisy is gone...." she trailed off, and I gulped. *Shit.* Dad told me that she died the last time I talked to him, which had been months ago. I didn't know she'd had a kid though.

"Well," I swallowed back the weird twisting of emotion that had settled in my throat. I'd read part of the situation wrong, but not all of it, "She's still pregnant." Maybe she hadn't been happily married for years, but she had still been involved with someone long enough to have a baby with them. And Rosie wasn't the reckless type. If she was pregnant, she was sure about getting that way.

Oma pursed her lips, disappointment in me for god-knows-what painted all over her face, as she handed me a chipped mug. Chocolatey steam floated up at my nose. The comforting smell sat disjointedly with the consternation I was feeling. "Also, not hers. Lily cannot carry a child. Lily and her Cameron and your *Röschen* made a plan. She is carrying *their* child."

I couldn't help it. My eyes went wide and I barely managed to keep myself from dropping my mug. I set it roughly on the table instead. Cocoa sloshed out over the edge. "Why would she do that? Oma, they could get an actual surrogate. And why aren't her parents or Lily taking care of Daisy's kid? Why is *Rosie* doing all this?"

"They cannot afford a surrogate. And Rosie cannot afford to care for Orion alone. Daisy left the poor child in Rosie's care. *Bärchen*, you know how her parents are. What the sisters were like together. Cameron and Rosie got married, temporarily, so his insurance would pay for the medical needs."

"Jesus Christ," I sat back, frowning and rubbing my palm over my face to hide the severity in my expression, "Oma, that's... That's insurance fraud. Isn't it?" Though, that was the least of what I was concerned about. Rosie *was* married, but it was some kind of transaction. That made no sense with what I remembered of my romantic, Hallmark-loving best friend. *The woman* I *wanted to marry.*

"They are paying her by feeding her and the boy and letting them live in a guest room," she continued, waving away my concern. "The money she makes here she saves for the school loans and for after the child is born. She does not think Lily will want her to stay."

"Oma," my voice broke. Of course, Lily wouldn't. Rosie would literally give her own body to help her sister and Lily would probably find some way to make Rosie feel like she owed *her* for it.

"The Farm, it does okay, but it is not enough," she continued ripping my world apart. But that's what I got for abandoning Rosie and doing the bare minimum to keep in touch with everyone else back home. "Rosie has big plans to help us grow, but she does not have much time, and we cannot pay her what she deserves." At that, her brow rose as if to say, *What are you going to do about it?*

Except, I had no idea. Rosie could have told me all this, but she didn't. At the very least, she could have corrected me when I called Orion her son. But she didn't. Five years and I'd gotten exactly what I deserved: she shut me out.

I had no idea what it would take to get her back.

I DRAGGED THE NEXT MORNING. Even more than usual. The nausea part of pregnancy had mostly subsided by that point, but I was having a flare-up. Probably because I hadn't eaten anything the night before. I couldn't stomach food after seeing Holden.

But I still managed to fumble together something close to my vision for the photo space at the main entrance before the farm opened. A few weeks into fall, I'd found a pretty wood and metal bench left on the side of the road, near one of the houses that had gone up for sale. Well, it wasn't necessarily *pretty* at the time, but it had potential. And Opa brought it back to life with a fresh coat of white paint and a few replaced wooden slats.

I'd also found an old mailbox at a junkyard, and Opa and I fixed that up, too, while Oma kept Orion busy making cookies last week. Now, the post had a candy cane spiral and the mailbox was glossy red. The perfect place to leave a letter for Santa.

I wanted to add a tree to the little scene, but settled for a few discreet posts that suspended sparkling Christmas lights. I'd stolen those from the house, but Oma said she didn't mind.

It was enough for now. It was cute and sweet and looked amazing with the old red truck, but was still a nice little spot when Opa needed it for deliveries.

I was standing back, admiring the work I'd been able to accomplish, and taking a few pictures to try and make work for social posts, when Oma walked up. Orion tagged along behind her, trying to munch on a cookie and keep his feet under him at the same time. I turned the camera on him and took another picture. This one just for me. *Maybe I'll leave it for Daisy, too.*

"It looks very good, *Röschen*," Oma praised, wrapping a surprisingly steady arm around my waist. She was a small old woman, but there was nothing frail about Oma Waldvogel. I hoped whatever kept her so strong would infuse through her touch.

I tucked myself into her arms a little deeper. Just in case. "Thanks, Oma," my whisper came out hoarse, a little on the side of tearful. *If the crying could stop any day now, that would be fantastic.*

She patted my arm and we watched Orion scramble onto the new bench. He turned around and grinned, chocolate smudges creasing all over his face. I took another picture.

"I need oranges. And star anise," Oma squeezed my arm one more time and stepped away, toward Ri, pulling a handkerchief from her apron. "Will you go to the big store? Opa will take Orion around the Farm and I will take care of the customers."

I sighed. *The big store* was the only store. And it was almost forty minutes away. Even that far, it managed to run the Duncans out of town. Or maybe they'd just seen the writing on the wall. The one I was desperately trying to rewrite.

But my lower back couldn't handle much more standing at that counter. Even *not* pregnant, it hurt. While supporting another entire human it had become almost impossible. "Yeah," I tucked my phone in my pocket, then stopped to kiss her and Ri on the cheeks, "I can do that. Call me if you think of anything else we need."

As much as I hated driving into the city, I didn't mind the errand. I didn't have to listen to the same squeaky voice singing the current favorite song of toddlers all over the world. I didn't have to pull over eight times because a toy had fallen out of reach. And I wasn't going to have to pry a stolen candy bar out of sticky fingers at the cash register. But that feeling of graciousness quickly turned to guilt.

I mean, I loved my nephew. But I was just so tired. This weird mix of babysitter and mother that I'd become was overwhelming. I wasn't Ri's mom, and I never would be. I didn't want to take Daisy away from him like that. He still asked for her sometimes. Instead, I'd become a different permanent fixture, not the one he always wanted, either. *Maybe it wouldn't be so hard if I wasn't alone.*

I groaned inwardly and rubbed my chest. Between the emotional ache and heartburn from pregnancy, I couldn't catch a break. But every station on the radio was playing Christmas music, so I felt like my guilt was being punished. My only choices were repetitive kiddie music or irritatingly optimistic holiday tunes. There was no winning. By the time I made it to the parking lot, I had more in common with the Grinch than Cindy Lou Who.

I didn't start to feel better until I made it into the store and the greeter smiled at me, then so did every customer I walked past. It was so refreshing to be anonymous. To not feel the weight of the Atwood curse echo with every step. I even managed to tune out ever-present carols as I lost myself in browsing the aisles. I only needed two things, but I decided to linger just a little bit. Not that I had time to linger, but I needed it. I needed to pretend. Just for a little while.

I was halfway through the store and nearing the spice aisle

when a mop of light brown hair caught my eye. My heart plummeted to my stomach. *Holden.* So much for being anonymous. I begged whatever entity was willing to help me that he wouldn't turn my way. I couldn't get out of the aisle in time. But apparently, even deities had it out for the Atwoods because he backed up and turned his cart down my row. I held my breath, then deflated. *It's not him.*

I realized my recollection was five years off. That shaggy style used to be Holden's signature. But when I'd seen him yesterday, his hair was cut short to his head. That stereotypical military cut. New hair, new man. But not the man I couldn't seem to fall out of love with. *And I've gone Grinch again.*

I gave up lingering and headed straight for the spices. The light feeling I'd managed to find had evaporated and was replaced with the crushing weight of what my life had become. I needed to get back to the Farm before there was no farm to get back to.

Of course, once I got to the spices, I couldn't find what I needed. Star anise wasn't incredibly common to find at grocery stores, but this store usually had a decent stock this time of year. I walked back and forth in front of the array twice before I pondered the idea of giving up. Then, just as quickly, I rejected it, because Oma didn't ask for much and there was no way I could let her down. Even for something so small.

I started another pass, this time much slower. I tried to get myself to focus. I was still whirling from the thought of seeing Holden. I'd just spotted it on one of the high shelves when I heard my name being yelled from the other end of the row.

I jumped, then spun around in the direction of the voice. A well-dressed man was rushing toward me and it took a second for my brain to register the face.

"Conrad?" Even to my own ears I sounded displeased and he frowned accordingly as he came to a stop in front of me. I wasn't meaning to be rude. I was just exhausted and I was finally someplace where no one knew me. Where I could finally take a break. Or I had been—until he showed up. So I hadn't meant to be rude, but I really did just want to be alone. I didn't want to continue the conversation by apologizing, so I just bit my lip and hoped he moved on.

But he didn't. Conrad squinted at me, his eyes traveling around my face. "Rosie," he started slowly, edging closer to me, "You don't seem well, babe."

I stepped back and waved my hand out to stop his approach, before rubbing my palm over my face. I didn't like that he felt so comfortable, but I probably did look questionably in charge of my faculties. He *had* scared the pants off me staring at spices.

"Rosie?" He tried again, coming forward and pressing his palms against my biceps. I guessed the gesture was meant to be comforting, but I didn't like it. I didn't want to be touched. Not by him. "I was going to stop by the Farm on my way back to see you."

"O-oh," I stuttered. His hands were rubbing up and down my arms. His body to close to mine. But everything about it felt wrong. The Christmas carols suddenly seemed too loud. A kid yelling in the next aisle over startled me.

Conrad's palm left my arm and came up to cup my jaw, "Babe?" His breath wafted over my face. He smelled like too spicy cinnamon gum. My eyes burned and my stomach revolted and that was finally enough to shake me free of the weird, uncomfortable paralysis I'd fallen into.

"I'm okay," I eked out a little space between us and felt like I could breathe again. "You need to finish your shopping," I glanced down and the curious mixture of products in his basket. It looked like a haphazard swiping of items off shelves. But maybe he'd just decided to make a dedicated trip to pick up those random things people always forget. "I'm all done now," I held up my own basket and dropped the star anise into it ceremoniously in a dramatic display to punctuate my point.

I forced a smile as I started to scoot around him. He didn't move, so I had to awkwardly shuffle close to the shelf. The aisles were too narrow, and even if I was barely showing, I still felt like I took up nearly the whole width. I'd just gotten past him when he stopped me again, "Wait!" He didn't yell, but it was still too loud for a grocery store. I cringed.

"Yeah?" I couldn't stop it from coming out on a sigh. I just wanted to get back to the farm, to Ri and Oma and Opa. As much as they reminded me of all the pain that was building up inside me, they were the best family I had. The only people who could make me feel at home,

"It was nice seeing you," he lowered his voice and reached toward me again. His hand hit my waist before I realized what he was going to do. But at the last second, I tucked my basket into my side to keep the embrace from being too close.

"You, too," I muttered the nicety I didn't mean and pushed away. I pivoted and rushed out of the aisle without looking back. I tried to tell myself it was nice to be wanted. But his persistence felt like too much. Or maybe it was just because he wasn't the man I'd always wanted to want me.

"Left, left," I grunted as my back hit roughly against the door jam. When Eric asked for my help moving a new water heater for the Inn, I hadn't expected the process to be quite so back-breaking. But even if I had known, he was letting me stay for next to nothing, so I felt I couldn't say no. And it wasn't like I had anything better to do. I didn't want to go back to the Farm until I had a plan to win Rosie back. Even just getting to be friends again. I wasn't sure things could get any worse, but I wasn't about to test that theory either.

"I *am* going left," I heard a matching strain in Eric's voice.

I tripped a little as the weight I was balancing shifted. The wrong direction. "My. Left," I gritted my teeth and tried to find my footing again.

"Why didn't you say that?" Eric groaned and then I felt the weight shift again, this time in a direction I could work with. I didn't bother to respond.

A few short, shuffled steps later, we'd gotten the huge heater in place. I only hoped it would be installed in time to have hot water again tonight. I'd just straightened up from trying to counter-stretch the new strain in my lower back when my stomach growled embarrassingly.

"Nothing like manual labor to kick up an appetite," Eric clapped me on the shoulder and moved around to the kitchen. I followed behind and caught him opening cabinet doors. "Shit," he slammed the last one and turned to me. I guessed he hadn't found anything.

"Or at least a beer," I muttered. It was still pretty early, but the heater was fucking heavy. The temperatures may have dropped below freezing outside, but it felt like summer inside.

"Yes," he pointed at me, then turned back to the fridge. I was glad *that* was already new. It looked even heavier and I didn't want to be the guy to have to help move it. "Or not," he grunted, his head still stuck in the fridge like something would appear if he just kept watch.

I leaned back against the door jam and shook my head, trying to keep my laugh inside. "It's all good, man," I finally said to break his spell, "Anything else you need?" Maybe I was avoiding the Rosie Problem, but I had no idea where to start. I was sort of hoping an idea would just come to me. Possibly while swinging a hammer at a nail I could imagine was myself for causing the problem to begin with.

"I can't ask for more, Moore, you've done more than a customer should already," Eric filled two glasses from the tap and slid one across the counter to me, smiling at the quasi-pun on my name.

I just shrugged, "Can't go back to the farm yet." No matter how badly I wanted to.

Eric laughed, "Ah, so you're just using me as an excuse to not fix things with your lady." I'd found myself giving him a very brief overview that morning while we'd taken out the old water heater and prepped the new one.

"She's got so much going on, so many reasons to feel overwhelmed. I have to make sure my turning up doesn't become just one more problem for her." That was the one conclusion I'd drawn that could actually make any of this make sense. Sweet little Rosie never held a grudge in her life, and while I definitely deserved her cold shoulder, it was completely unlike her to let me believe a lie and then run away.

She should have called me on my shit the second she saw me. But she hadn't. And the only reasonable conclusion I could muster up was that she just couldn't. I was sure Oma had only given me part of the story, and that was bad enough. If I was going to get her back, I'd have to find a way to do it without adding to her burden.

Eric hummed and if I hadn't been wearing steel-toed boots, I would have stepped on my own foot. It had taken less than twenty-four hours to realize that Eric Wilder was Pinesbury's Charlie Anderson. He had a way of looking at someone and waiting for an answer that demanded nothing less than the comprehensive truth.

"Anyway," I said before Eric could dig any deeper into my head, "I need to eat before I even attempt those conversations." I tried to say it lightly, jokingly. But the truth was, I was a little nauseous. I wasn't sure food would help, but it would buy time. "Let's go grab a bite somewhere," I offered, pulling my keys from my pocket and tossing them in the air.

Eric smiled, half nodded, then shook his head, "Nope. Can't leave. I'm having security cameras installed today and they gave me one of those wide-ass service windows. I have to be here to make sure it's all set up right."

"Security cameras?" I squinted. I was pretty sure there were only like ten people left in this town. Well, maybe that was an exaggeration. But still, I didn't remember any occasions that would have warranted security cameras.

I was answered with an irritated grunt. But after my

confused stare, Eric finally explained, "You weren't here to see it, but about half of the old businesses on Main Street were dealing with regular vandalism before they finally shut down. And a buddy of mine bought a house two towns over because his real estate agent told him similar things were happening to private properties in Pinesbury, too."

My eyebrows went up in shock.

"If you ask me," he continued, "someone is up to something. Probably one of those big developers that have been taking over towns like this all over the state. I'm not taking any chances, and I'm not letting some city scum force me out either."

I nodded. It made sense to me. But I hated to think that my beloved hometown was the victim of a deliberate attempt to sabotage and ruin it. Granted, in retrospect, I could see how it was a good target. Still, my stomach churned again wondering if this was something else I could have prevented. Had I just stayed.

And I wondered, too, if that was part of Rosie's stress. Pinesbury may not have loved the Atwoods, but no one loved Pinesbury more than Rosie. I bounced my keys in my hand as I pondered the idea. If I could figure out if there was any truth to Eric's supposition, maybe I could do something to stop it. And maybe win Rosie back in the process.

Eric's head cocked, noticing my slip into thought. He opened his mouth to speak, but I cut him off, "I'll find us some lunch. And beer. Back soon." I turned and left before he could respond.

My first plan was to go down to Rowe's Tavern. With the old diner gone and the rest of Main Street shuttered, it was probably the only place that still served food in a forty-minute radius. In high school, I might not have thought twice about it. It was cool to be somewhere so shady. Edgy. We didn't even need a very good fake to be served, despite the fact that Donny Hooper knew all of us from town. He just didn't give a shit. Which was great when we were fifteen and didn't know better.

But I'd had a lot of time to spend on memories over the years, and my recollections of Pinesbury, while mostly filtered through the rose-colored glasses that had confused Frazier, shifted to reality quickly when it came to the only bar in town. It didn't take long before I realized that what we saw there wasn't typical of the kind of place someone would want to brag about going to.

It reeked of smoke, even though the Fire Marshall had demanded customers stop smoking inside. But why would they when Hooper still did? There wasn't a single night that passed without a bar fight. Usually, there'd be two. The cops never showed up. It wasn't the fine folks of Pinesbury fighting, either. Well, not entirely. Rowe's Tavern attracted the worst from all the neighboring towns. Sometimes even from the city. That was probably why it was the one place still surviving. It was the only one that didn't subsist entirely on locals. So when the locals left, the doors could stay open.

As I drove through town, I pondered if I really wanted to make the stop at the Tavern. It was the one place that *should* have closed, and I wasn't sure I wanted to be a reason it could stay open. Not that I thought I could make that much difference. But my time overseas had made me more discretionary. Had taught me the significance that one person, one decision, could have.

I slowed as I approached the turn, still debating, and what I witnessed made up my mind. Around the side of the bar, I could see Hooper standing outside with someone. His feet were braced apart and his hands were alternating between sitting stiffly on his hips and flying aggressively up into the air. Fifty feet later, and I could see the figure he was arguing with.

It took me a second to recognize Becca Rowe-Hooper. She'd been two grades below Rosie and I so we hadn't interacted much, but I did remember her being a shy, mousey thing. I would have imagined her being more likely to run away from an argument than stand her ground. But times had changed. Becca was still small, but there was nothing mouse-like about her anymore. Her face was bright red and it looked like she was having none of whatever Hooper was spitting at her.

I gripped the steering wheel with so much force I thought it'd snap into pieces when I saw Hooper step forward aggressively, his hand swinging into the air as if he were about to strike his daughter.

I stopped right in the middle of the street. The creaky break noise caught Hooper's attention and he turned, hands on his hips to squint at me. He needed glasses because I could make out their expressions just fine. I ignored his glare and looked past him to Becca. She obviously recognized me, but she shook her head. *Fuck.* I almost turned in the lot anyway. Like hell I'd let him treat her that way, didn't matter that she was his kid.

But she mouthed, "No," and shook her head firmly again, spreading her hands out in front of her to gesture the matter was not up for debate. Based on her stance and the look in her eye, this was nothing she wasn't used to handling. Still, guilt tore a knot in my stomach as I drove away. I promised myself I'd find a way to check in with her while her dad wasn't around.

In for a penny, in for a pound. I guessed I was planning on fixing things for the whole damn town. I stepped on the gas and started the trek to the city.

I stomped through the grocery store a little grumpier than I'd woken up. I thought I'd figured out a plan to win Rosie back, but it came with the realization that everything I'd missed so much overseas was gone. It was halfway out the door when I'd left, and it slipped through my fingers entirely because I didn't see it.

On my way back to the cold storage, I had to shuffle around a basket of random items that had been left in the middle of the spice aisle. I froze, then looked back on it angrily. Someone had come in, filled a basket with what looked like nothing significant, and then just dumped it. Decided they didn't want it and didn't even attempt to put anything back.

I scowled. There was no way I could let the city invade my town. Not when these were the kind of people it brought. I turned on my heel and marched to the back of the store, grabbing a case of beer and two frozen pizzas. Feeling grouchier by the minute and ready to get the hell out of the city.

One thing was for sure, I'd have to exorcise the Grinch in my soul before I saw Rosie tonight. Even if it could only be for an hour. And I did my best for the rest of the afternoon. The security company was leaving as I pulled up to the Inn. We ate and wrenched around the old building, and I picked Eric's brain about the goings-on in town since I'd been gone. He'd been around long enough to see it deteriorate. To watch as family after family took their leave. He'd tried to make a point to visit the business still there, to encourage them to stay, but one by one, they all left. Until the only families left with any meaningful ties at all were mine and the Rowe-Hoopers.

The news wasn't good, but the information was. I was feeling significantly more chipper by the time I cleaned up and jumped in the truck. I'd do some investigating on my own and I had a plan in place. Something I could spend my time on. Something I could do for Rosie. And that was the best feeling in the world.

But it was no use. Rosie was gone by the time I made it to

the farm. Oma said she had a doctor's appointment and left early. I stayed for dinner and obligingly carried leftovers back for Eric. As I drove away, I thought I saw lights coming heading up toward the main entrance. Slowly, and not from the road. I stopped the truck and squinted at the trees. *Nothing.* After a physically and emotionally exhausting day, I was losing my mind.

rosie

"Oma, Oma, Oma," Orion chanted from the backseat, bouncing his stuffed bear in his lap to punctuate his words. He'd been upset when I made him leave early with me yesterday. Carrying a crying toddler into a doctor's appointment wasn't my idea of a good time, but I was too worried that I'd run into Holden if I had to come pick up Ri after the appointment.

The trip to the store had eaten up some hours, and leaving early cut my chances of seeing him even more. But I knew I was pushing my luck. Oma had gently scolded me yesterday for letting Holden believe that Orion was my son and that I'd well and truly moved on. I knew she meant well, but my fragile heart couldn't take much more.

It wasn't like I didn't miss him. *God,* I missed him so much. I'd missed him for five long years. But he'd cut *me* off. And how could I trust him to be back now? How could I trust that he wouldn't just run away again? I just couldn't take that risk. Not right now. Not with so much on my plate, so many lives dependent on me. I couldn't afford another heartbreak.

And it was with that last thought on my mind that I rolled up to the main entrance of Waldvogel Farms, intending to drop

Orion off closer to the little cottage where I knew Oma would be preparing for early morning customers. I'd go park around back after. It was my way of coping with the guilt of taking him from his favorite people early because I was too chicken to face my former best friend.

Opa came running out before I could even pull into a parking space, waving his arms and looking entirely too unhappy about seeing us. More than a little concerned, I scrambled out of the car, leaving it half in a spot.

"Opa—" I started to yell at him.

He cut me off, "Rosie! Oh, Rosie, you did not get Oma's call?" He stopped abruptly in front of me, cupping my elbows and positioning his body as if he were trying to block my path.

I glanced back over my shoulder to my car. My phone was probably dead, I'd been too exhausted to put on the charger last night. I'd only had two percent left when I tossed it into my bag this morning. "N-no..." I stuttered, "I think it's dead. Is everything okay?"

My stomach dropped in fear. Something was obviously very wrong, but Opa looked okay standing in front of me. And if Oma was supposed to have called, then she was okay, too, right? So what could be wrong?

"You should go home," Opa interrupted my tumultuous thoughts with another that didn't do anything to make me feel better. What could be *this* wrong?

"Why?" I looked back again to glimpse Orion. The little boy could obviously sense the gravity of the situation and was chewing his lip and staring at Opa and me, his toy forgotten in his lap. "Opa, what's wrong?" I turned back to my honorary grandfather.

He shook his head and pulled me into a tight, unexpected hug. I didn't doubt that he loved me, loved Orion, but he wasn't a touchy man. "I am so sorry, Rosie. I hoped you would not come, so you would not see."

"See *what*, Opa?" I felt like I couldn't breathe, and I was suddenly grateful for his break in character because I wasn't sure I could keep myself standing without his arms around me. My mind raced a million miles a minute. Had there been a fire? *No,* I'd have seen the signs of that. *So, what?*

"There was a break-in last night," Opa finally stopped the train of what-ifs with an answer. "No, that is not the right word. There was no theft."

"What?" I leaned back and shook my head. A break-in with no theft? That didn't sound bad at all. Didn't warrant any of this. Probably a teenage attempt at romanticism, breaking into a tree farm near Christmas. We could handle broken locks and a little mess.

But Opa still looked grim. "Vandals. At the cottage."

My chest seized, but I couldn't speak. A couple of years ago, there had been a rash of break-ins and vandalism at the businesses in town, and some of the homes, too. I'd been away at school, but my parents and the Waldvogels told me about it. They'd been seemingly endless. It got so bad that most of the businesses left. And when there was no one to clean up the mess, to create another blank slate, the vandals left. We'd all just assumed they'd found someone else to torment.

"I am very sorry, Rosie. Your display..." He let the rest of the sentence hang and I could have thrown up to fill the void. Insurance could pay for the damage, but the monetary value wasn't the issue. It wasn't much, it wasn't that it was a huge cost. But I'd worked so hard on it. I'd salvaged so much, spent so much *time*.

And time was the one thing I couldn't get back. I'd already posted that the photogenic little setup was ready. The feedback had been phenomenal. I was sure we'd see an uptick in visitors this week. I'd planned on making a small concessions order today, so we'd have hot chocolate and coffee to offer for people who came by just for the pictures. It wouldn't drastically increase our profits, but it would be proof of concept. And I could put that in my proposal.

I was so lost in my spiraling thoughts that I hadn't even realized Opa had been slowly shuffling me backward until he deposited me into the driver's seat.

"'Tee-Ro. Cold," Orion's voice fully broke the spell.

I twisted around to peer into the back seat and tried to blink away any tears before he could see them. I felt Opa step away and saw him round the car as I spoke to Ri, "Sorry, buddy, we'll get you inside in just a minute. I bet Oma will make you pancakes for breakfast." I hoped she would. I was expecting Holden to be the source of my next heartbreak, not *this*. I needed a minute.

The door next to Ri opened and Opa reached in, unbuckling and pulling him from his car seat while chatting about what he would like on his pancakes. I took a breath.

"Take Orion to Oma, I will move the car," Opa ordered, coming back around with my nephew in his arms. I hesitated, looking back for Ri's bag, but decided it could wait. I had to spend whatever mental energy I had preparing myself to walk past the damage. If I hadn't come this way, I at least could have avoided it until I was alone.

"Oh, no!" Orion yelped as we approached what used to be my bench and mailbox. He pushed back against my chest and stared wide-eyed at me, "Happened?"

I gulped and glanced back over the scene. Opa had been trying to clean it up, but the destruction was too bad. The mailbox was totally destroyed. Broken from the post and misshapen, probably from being beaten by a bat. The iron side rails of the bench had escaped mostly unscathed, just chipped paint, but the wooden slats were unsalvageable.

The truck still looked drivable, but the paint was horribly scratched. I looked in the back and found the remnants Opa had cleaned up already. Shredded lights and pieces of broken poles were scattered on top of a thin, fresh layer of snow.

I walked around the truck, still not answering Orion's question. I expected to find slashed tires. Something more significant. This truck was the non-human face of the business, but it had just been keyed. I sighed in relief. I remembered that one of the biggest challenges the businesses faced a few years ago was that the damage was never significantly high in a monetary sense. Insurance just paid it out and the understaffed Sheriff's office didn't bother to investigate when the cost of the damage was so low.

Hoping that trend would hold true, I shifted Orion up higher on my hip, trying to pull his leg to a more comfortable spot around my growing belly. Slowly, the cottage came into view from behind a patch of trees. I'd planned to string lights on these trees soon, as a way of showing off the merchandise and directing traffic to the little building where customers could purchase their trees—and concessions.

All those thoughts went out the window, though, as I approached. Hapless graffiti had been sprayed around the outside of the building. It didn't even say anything, didn't signify anything. It was just stark black destructive lines on the beautifully faded red paint. Orion gasped again.

The glass window we opened to take sales through had been shattered. I stopped long enough to look inside. There were small patches of snow, where the flurries from the night had blown in. Every cabinet and drawer was open. Contents spilled through the room, littering every inch of the floor.

I stopped at the bank every day when I left, so I wasn't

worried about the cashbox. There would have only been a little bit of money inside, just enough to make change for the first customers.

But money wasn't the issue. Insurance would pay for it. It would pay for the window, and the paint, and the truck, and the lights. But it wouldn't clean up this mess. It wouldn't reorganize the files, it wouldn't rebuild the bench, or find a new mailbox.

We couldn't open today. Maybe not even tomorrow. I swallowed the well of tears building in my throat. Anxiety built like a raging blizzard inside my chest. Blinding, suffocating. I turned and hurried along the path to the house.

Sitting on the floor of the cottage sorting shuffled papers, I was grateful Oma had taken one look at me and plucked Orion from my arms. Promising all the fixings he requested for his pancakes. I didn't care that he'd probably be in a sugar coma by noon. He was happy, he wasn't thinking about what happened. *At least he can still believe in Christmas.*

I was also grateful Oma didn't pressure me too hard to stay and eat, too. I wasn't sure I could even stomach it. But she did bring out a plate of buttered toast while Orion was eating his breakfast. It was still sitting on the messy desk, though the baby had won a little and I'd taken a few bites.

Calming music was playing on my phone, now plugged in next to my abandoned toast. I tried to take deep breaths and move slowly as I repaired what I could. All this stress and anxiety probably wasn't good for the little niece or nephew I was growing. I thought about calling my sister or her husband for help, but I was sure my sister would tell me just to walk away. That it wasn't worth it.

But the farm was the only bit of happy memories I had left. No one would love it and fix it like Oma, Opa, and I would. It meant too much to me to just walk away. *I'm not Holden*, I scoffed to myself. Then jumped when I heard a knock on the doorjamb.

I twisted my body around too quickly and pinched something deep inside that angered the baby. I heaved as the cramping feeling slowly passed and pressed my hands against my stomach. The pain ebbed and my vision cleared and I finally processed the sight of the visitor at the door. *Freaking Conrad.* Our last meeting had unsettled me, and now I was feeling decidedly less welcoming to his advances.

"Are you... Pregnant?" The way he said the word, you'd think it had poisoned him. And it obviously wasn't what he'd come to discuss if he was only noticing now. *It startled him.* If that discovery was enough to distract him from what he needed, I probably didn't want to know anyway. *Probably just after another date.*

"Yes," I rolled my eyes as I attempted to stand up. I almost explained the situation, but held my tongue when he didn't make a move to help me and instead stepped back like I was infectious. "What do you need, Conrad? There's a lot going on here right now." He was mistaken if he thought he was going to get me to agree to dinner now. Not with everything going on and the way he'd just looked at me.

He coughed when he caught my irritated glare. "I, uh, didn't realize you were seeing anyone..."

I shuffled over to the desk and kept my back on him, attempting to neaten the pile of papers I'd stood up with. "I'm not, I'm a surrogate," I gave into giving the briefest explanation in the hopes he'd leave. I debated if I even cared that he still hadn't gotten a tree yet.

"Oh, that's good," he spoke up behind me. His voice

sounded relieved, but still not quite happy.

Confused, I turned back to him. His expression didn't clear anything up and, feeling more discomforted, I rushed to move the conversation along. Subconsciously rubbing my belly. "We're closed today. Obviously. But if you had a tree picked out already, I can have Opa mark it and deliver it…"

"No, uh," his expression suddenly cleared like he'd made up his mind and stepped further into the small room, crowding me, "I heard about the break-in. I wanted to help." He lowered his voice and pressed closer to me with the last sentence. The smell of cinnamon gum on his breath overwhelmed me again and I fought against the wave of nausea.

"How?" I asked, slipping away from the desk with my papers and pretending to hunt down where they went in the file cabinet.

Conrad moved closer, his front nearly pressed against my back, and his hands rubbing up my arms. "Oh, Rosie," his voice was thick with pity that itched against my confidence, "You posted about it, remember? On the Farm social pages. To explain the closure."

"Right," I sighed, fighting the urge to escape again. It felt too rude, though I didn't know why I cared. It wasn't like he was being polite deliberately missing my hints.

"You need to rest, babe," he whispered, his face inching closer to my ear. "I know some contractors I can call to take care of this. Call it a Christmas gift. And I'm assuming Mrs. Wald-vogel has the kid. Let me take you home."

I appreciated the offer to help, especially knowing we couldn't afford the window until the insurance paid out and we still would probably have to install it ourselves because of the cost. But he called Orion "the kid," despite knowing his name. And that hit me in all the wrong places.

I was overwhelmed, and tired, and pregnant, and suddenly

ravenous from putting off breakfast. There was nothing I could do to stop the anger from spewing out. I felt hot enough to melt every inch of snow on the Farm when I turned on Conrad and pushed him roughly back.

He stared at me in shock, then moved to take a step toward me again. I could see that he was barely controlling his anger as well. At me, for pushing him away. But he still wasn't going to give in and I was exhausted.

"No," I held out one hand to stop him and braced the other behind me on the cabinet. "Thank you," I enunciated the words carefully, "But, no."

"Rosie," the grin he plastered on was meant to be charming, but it just felt slimy.

"Enough, Conrad," I cut him off. "*Orion*," I emphasized his name, "and this Farm are my number one priorities. I appreciate your interest, but I don't have the time or energy to return it. And the fact that you can't seem to take a hint is not helping."

Conrad sputtered, his face turning red and flustered. Like he'd never been rejected before and had no idea how to deal with it.

Not that we could afford it, but feeling like I needed it, I spoke again to finish with, "I think you'd better get your tree somewhere else."

His expression turned hard. He opened his mouth to speak, but then thought better of it. He turned and marched out of the small office without a glance back.

I sighed and eased myself into the desk chair. *Freaking Conrad.* Conrad *and* Holden.

Why do men always think they have a right to butt in?

MY PHONE RANG mid-morning and woke me up. I'd struggled to fall asleep between thoughts of Rosie and the demise of Pinesbury, but finally managed it around three a.m. Now, my phone going off was entirely unwelcome. I reached blindly for it, prepared to impart the full wrath of my grump on whoever answered.

I stopped, though, when I heard Opa's voice before I managed to get a word out. "Holden," my name sounded just as stilted coming from him as it did when Oma said it, "There were vandals at the Farm last night. I need you to come help with the cleaning."

"Shit," I scrambled out of bed faster than I did when alarms warned us of incoming mortars. Eric had just told me about the vandalism issues yesterday, and he had said they'd happened a while ago and stopped. What were the chances they started up again last night? And at the Farm in particular? It hadn't been a target before. Neither had the Inn or Rowe's. "On my way."

I hung up and pulled on my jeans and boots and stormed out the door with the questions on my mind. And the memory of the lights peeking through the trees as I drove away was right there with them. There was only one place I knew I could go to get the information without a huge explanation. I dialed Charlie as I jumped in the truck and cranked the old engine.

He answered after the third ring, "Holden!"

"Hey, man," I started roughly, interrupting his greeting. I'd only spoken six words so far that morning and they'd all been laced with anxiety.

"Let me guess, you hate it and you're on your way to D.C. to beg for a job? Not sure I can help. It has been a whole two days since I heard from you."

"Fuck you," I laughed at my friend's joking. It wasn't uproarious, but it was honest. I appreciated that he was always ready to bring the balance. Levity when needed, or a level head.

"Ah, well, I tried," I heard his chuckle breaking through the static of my speakerphone. "You sound like you need something. What's up?" And there was the level head.

Now I was quiet for a moment, trying to figure out exactly what I needed from him. I gripped the steering wheel beneath my palms.

I spent too long thinking and Charlie spoke up again, "Holden?"

"I'm here. I'm just not sure how to explain it," I hesitated. "Something's going on in town. I don't know what, don't know what to look for..."

I heard a thunk that I imagined was Charlie tipping back and propping his feet up on a desk, "So, what makes you think there is something going on at all?"

"The guy who runs the Inn, Eric Wilder, told me about a string of vandalisms a few years ago," I gave Charlie all the information that Eric had given me on the short drive to the Farm. Including his theory about deliberate sabotage by a developer.

Charlie hummed after I finished. "That's all bad news,

Holden, but it sounds like it's all over. What do you want to do about it now?"

"They started again, at the Farm last night," I answered flatly.

"Shit," Charlie mirrored my response to Opa just twenty minutes before.

"I'm on my way to check it out now. Almost there. I was going to call around to some old neighbors today, but I don't know where else to start. I have to figure it out, though. There's too much at stake, I can't let..." I stopped abruptly before I mentioned Rosie.

But I didn't have to say her name for Charlie to get the gist. I heard the line crackle in the intense silence that followed. "Okay," he finally spoke, "I'll see what we can find. Carter's a magician with shit like this. Send me pictures of the damage."

"Yep," I pulled up at the main entrance, figuring I'd find Opa on that side of the lot. "And thanks, Charlie."

I heard his, "No problem," right before the click of the call ending.

After taking a minute to catch my breath and steel my emotions—the last thing I wanted was to show up angry and spewing and add to Rosie's plate—I headed for the row of trees and old wooden archway that marked the entrance to the Farm. I glanced around looking for signs of damage, but while the signage was old and the paint chipped, it looked exactly as it had two days ago.

I kept going and caught my first glimpse of the night's disfigurement. I hadn't seen Rosie's display in person yet, but I'd seen her post yesterday. I hoped she'd want to show it to me in person last night, but she hadn't been there and I decided to wait. Now I wouldn't get a chance. The whole thing had been destroyed. Opa had picked up most of it, by the looks of it. Piled up in the old red truck.

I winced as I ran my fingers across the deep grooves in the paint. Looking through the window, I saw the iron side rails of the bench that had been in the picture sitting on the passenger seat. I guessed those were the only things that could be saved.

Sighing, I pushed on toward the cottage. On my way, I caught sight of a man stomping through the trees, angrily rushing toward the main parking lot. I recognized him by his coat as the man I'd seen kissing Rosie the other night. My fists flexed involuntarily. I knew now that she wasn't involved with him, but I didn't like him sniffing around either. Not that I had any right to stake a claim when I was still trying to win back just her friendship.

Then as he got closer, I recognized the man as the teenager I once knew him as. "Conrad?" I halted in disbelief. Then irritation. He'd been sniffing around Rosie in particular as long as I could remember. It wasn't like I'd ever *really* interfered if she wanted to date someone in high school. We both did, though not seriously. But I never liked Conrad. And I especially didn't like him showing up now.

He was obviously pissed, but when he heard me his expression morphed into a vacant smile. Then he recognized me, and it morphed again into annoyed disgust. He stopped in front of me and looked me over, obviously judging what he saw. "Didn't know you were back in town, Moore."

"Only been a couple days. Came to see Rosie," I nodded toward where he'd been coming from. I couldn't help myself. I staked the claim that wasn't mine to stake. But while the years may have been good for Conrad's wardrobe, based on the shiny shoes and designer snow coat, his scowl told me they'd nothing for his personality.

He scoffed and glanced over his shoulder, "Good luck with that."

"What—" I started to ask what he meant by that, but he'd already pushed past me, continuing toward the parking lot.

Shaking my head, I moved on. If he was that pissed, Rosie had probably already told him off. Nothing more I needed to do about *that* problem. Now I just had to hope she'd see me.

I found her, head pressed into her palms, sitting in the desk chair in the sales cottage. The place was destroyed, though it looked like Rosie had spent some time cleaning it up. Most of the glass shards had made it into a pile in the corner. There were stacks of paper spread around the room. There was nothing she could do about the paint streaking the outside though.

"Hey, *Röschen*," I kept my voice low as I eased deeper into the tiny space.

Her head jolted up so quickly and she spun around in the chair so fast, I couldn't stop myself from taking a step forward to catch her if she fell. As I got closer, though, she reeled back and slammed the chair into the desk, scattering a pile of paper. She groaned down at the mess of paper, then turned her glare on me.

"Don't. Call. Me. That," I hadn't expected her to sound so angry and I fell back to give her room. She stood up and followed after me, a finger pointing accusingly. "You have no right, Holden. You left. You should've just stayed gone."

"I got out, Rosie. And Opa just called, told me what happened. I'm here to help," I tried, moving forward until she was jabbing into my chest. I tried to keep the rest of my body language neutral, though. Tried to show her that it was okay, I was okay with her anger. Knew I deserved it. But that didn't mean I would give up.

"We don't need your help, Holden," she spat, stepping away again. "Opa, Oma, and I have been doing just fine without you. And we'll continue to do so when you leave again, too."

Her words hit like a knife to the gut. Sharp and plunging deep. Twisting until I felt my insides tear apart. "I'm not leaving, *Rö*—Rosie," I caught myself on the nickname, but couldn't help taking another hesitant half-step toward her.

"No," and I heard her voice break, my promise to stay only making things worse, "I can't stop you from seeing your grandparents. But I've got *this* under control." She didn't trust me, didn't trust that I'd realized what a mistake I'd made and had every intention of fixing it.

All I needed to do was make her understand, "I mean it, Rosie. I'm here. For whatever you need." She didn't look at me while I spoke, though. And she made sure to keep her distance. Her hands absentmindedly rubbing over her growing belly, and I couldn't help but feel jealous of it. She was a surrogate for her sister. But still, *what if she wasn't?* What if I had missed my chance? My chest burned.

Finally, she lifted her chin. "I need you to go, Holden. Please," her eyes filled with tears as she begged for me to listen. To hear her and do what she asked.

I didn't want to. But I also didn't want to be another problem for her—another thing she had to deal with. I glanced down at her stomach again. She was already dealing with too much. "Let me just see what Opa needed," I hesitated. I could get out of her hair, but still be close. Help wherever he needed me. Then he could take some of her burdens at the Farm.

"No, Holden," and I wanted to gouge out my own eyeballs watching her first tears tip over. *I did that. I caused those.* Her head shook gently, "Not today. I can't do it today."

I gulped and nodded. My throat felt tight, like I could barely get the air down. Every part of me wanted to go to her, to hold her. I needed to be there for her, but she needed me gone. I turned and stepped back outside. The chill in the air matched the ice I felt inside. The empty Farm and vacant winter left room for the echoes of my mistake to ring in my ears. I felt hollow inside.

But this was Christmas. And deep down, I knew Rosie still loved it. Still believed in the miracle of Christmas. I'd just have to make her see it again. I'd help her. And the Farm. But not today. Today, I'd walk away again. Like she'd asked. But this was the last damn time. I'd be back again tomorrow, and I wasn't going to take no for an answer. Well, not entirely. She could ignore me if she wanted to, but I'd help wherever I could.

I found Opa on the way out and told him my plan. He agreed to tape up the window for the day with an old tarp from the barn until I could come back tomorrow with a new window and plenty of paint. *This will be my most important mission yet.* I smiled as the corny thought filtered through my mind.

It wasn't wrong, though.

On my way back to town, I diverted down Main Street. Even with a plan, I was frustrated that Rosie wouldn't let me help right away. It meant one more day before the Farm could open back up. But I understood it. Understood the need for time to process. And it wasn't like she was running away like I had all those years ago. She'd still been cleaning up, dealing with the mess. So what if she decided that the *Me* part of her problems needed to wait? At least she was still there. Still facing it all.

The extra trek gave me time to think and I wanted to explore the old businesses as well. See if there'd been any new signs of damage or vandalism. If the motive was to run businesses out of town, the closed-up shops shouldn't have any new damage. After all, why waste time and risk being found out when there was nothing to be gained?

Eric spotted me on his way back to the Inn from wherever.

The city, based on his direction, but I hadn't seen him that morning so I had no idea what he had been working on. I was halfway down the street, and so far my theory had held. I'd stalked around every building, tested every door, and looked in every window. Each one was in various stages of disarray, some sported graffiti or other obvious damage from vandals, but nothing looked recent. Debris was still buried under thick layers of snow.

"Thought you were at the Farm?" He pulled over and called from his truck window while I was testing the knob on another door. *Locked.*

I turned around and walked up to him, leaning against his door. "Was. Rosie asked me to leave."

He whistled while I just shook my head, "Tough, but what the hell are you doing here?"

"Vandals got the Farm last night," I filled him in on what I'd seen. "Thought I'd see if there was anything new around here. I didn't hear anything at the Inn last night."

Eric shook his head this time, "Nope. All good there, guess I got the cameras in right on time."

I nodded and glanced down the street toward the buildings I hadn't checked out yet. "I'll finish up and head back and help you out. Could use the distraction." I needed to pick his brain about window installations, too. The last thing I wanted was to fuck it up and create a new problem for Rosie.

Eric responded by cutting the engine on his truck and making to step out. I stood back so he could. "Nah, I'll help *you* out. I'm ahead of schedule after yesterday," he chuckled, slapping me on the back and heading toward the next building. I wasn't sure that was true. Eric had closed for the season to do one big push of renovations, after making due for the last several years and saving up, but he had to open by Spring if he wanted to *stay* open.

I knew him well enough by now to know it wouldn't do any good to remind him of that fact, though. So I accepted his help and promised myself I'd spend as much time returning the favor as I could. Just as soon as I fixed things with Rosie.

"Nothing," Eric came around the corner of the last vacant shop, dusting powdery snow off his gloved hands.

"Same," I sighed, coming to stand next to him and staring off at the last stop. It wasn't one I was necessarily interested in making, but it needed to be done: Rowe's Tavern. I still needed to check on Becca, but I could see Hooper's car parked along the side of the building and it wouldn't do any good to ask questions in front of him.

I stood, hands on my hips staring at the building until Eric broke me from my stupor. "Next stop?" He asked. Glancing over, I saw he had the same hesitant expression I did. But he gave a half shake of his head and started toward the bar.

"You ever been here before?" I asked Eric as we crunched across the gravel. Christmas lights were strung haphazardly across the roofline, but almost a third of them were out. Decorations blinked in the window, half dead. It gave the place a more eerie than festive feel.

Eric grunted, "Once. No good reason to come back."

I mimicked the sound and stopped at the door. Halting to take a breath before pulling it open. *Here goes nothing.*

Dust motes swirled around, barely visible through the fractured sunlight that managed to make its way into the dark bar. The smell of beer and smoke hung thickly in the air and I fought the urge to cough. Eric didn't. His hacking made an impolite racket, but then, this place deserved it.

As my eyes adjusted to the dank darkness, three figures

came into view. Hooper was standing behind the bar, half-heartedly drying a glass. Then an older woman. She glanced our way and I recognized Mrs. Danforth's glare. Then the last person turned and...*fucking Conrad. Great.*

"Well, well," Hooper started, his sneer barely visible in the room, but I could sure hear it. "If it isn't Pinesbury's Golden Boy. Did ya get tired of the desert?"

"Donny," I ignored his questioning jab and settled on his name as a greeting. As I approached the bar, I felt Eric slowly stepping up behind me. Braced. I wasn't anticipating a fight, but I guessed that was just the vibe from any interaction in this place. I stopped outside of arm's length from the trio and cleared my throat. "The Farm had some issues last night, I was just wondering if you did as well?"

Hooper chuckled humorlessly, "Why? You gonna show them what a big, bad soldier can do?"

I cringed. How could we have ever thought this place was cool? Not that we'd *liked* Hooper back then. Obviously, we could forgive a lot if it meant access to alcohol.

"We'll take that as a no, then," Eric spoke up before I could.

"You having problems yourself, Wilder?" Conrad addressed Eric. It hadn't crossed my mind that the two might have been acquainted, but apparently they were. And apparently, it wasn't an amicable relationship. "Maybe you should just give in and sell?"

"The Inn's doing great, Clarke," Eric answered him dryly. "No problems."

Mrs. Danforth scoffed and Eric turned to her, "Something on your mind, ma'am?" The words were polite enough, but the tone said Eric knew something about her as well.

She raised a grizzled hand and pointed a finger at me, "If you're looking for the source of trouble, I suggest you look at your lodger, Mr. Wilder. Mr. Moore always did have a destructive streak. And didn't I see you driving down from that way last night?" She finished with a snide smile at me, like she'd just won something.

I rolled my eyes and nudged Eric's shoulder, turning to leave. He glared a second longer, then followed after. As I pushed the door open, I groaned, "One broken window when I was ten years old and I'll never live it down."

Eric's laugh was half chuckle, half shudder. And I didn't blame him. I hadn't seen Becca, so I'd have to go back at least one more time and I was already dreading the experience. Part of me was tempted to take up the flag of the vandals in the hopes of running Hooper out of town. If it wouldn't have hurt Rosie, I might have.

We'd made it to the edge of the lot when I heard the door slam shut again. I looked back to see Conrad leaving the bar. He stepped out into the sun and squinted, searching until his eyes landed on us. His gaze lingered too long, his lips curled into a derisive grin.

A sick feeling swirled in my stomach. Ominous. Warning. The kind of feeling that used to have me checking my rifle and sleeping with one eye open. My gaze swept back up the street, to the vacant shops and careless attempt at decorating on the street lights lining the road. I could admit that I'd exaggerated the merits of my hometown over the last five years, but I knew for a fact it hadn't been this bad.

My gut told me Eric was right. This had been deliberate. And one thing was for sure: I was going to find out what the hell was going on in Pinesbury.

FIVE DAYS after the break-in there still hadn't been another incident. I also hadn't managed to find another mailbox, but I was starting to breathe easier. Despite the fact that Holden had been at the Farm. Every. Single. Day.

I wasn't sure how I felt about that. Opa and Oma were thrilled, and I should have been, too. We'd only needed to be closed for two days because of his help. He and Opa had even been able to rebuild the bench. It was sitting in its pride of place at the front of the Farm. No mailbox, obviously, but a few wooden milk crates had appeared stacked securely together and painted red in its place. A perfect spot for resting cups of hot cocoa.

I had a sneaking suspicion about who was behind the crates. And I suspected the same person was behind the boxes on boxes of Christmas lights that appeared in the cottage this morning. Some had already been strung on the repaired bench display, but there were piles more waiting. I'd mentioned to Oma that I wanted to pick some up, but hadn't gone into detail about where I planned to put them. If I had, I was sure they would have already been in place.

It was too much and not enough. Or maybe it was just right. I couldn't tell, couldn't decide if it meant something or if I was just getting carried away. Falling back into old patterns of believing in Christmas miracles. Despite the work that needed to be done, I made excuses to keep away from the Farm whenever I could. Proximity to Holden Moore fogged my mind, and I needed a clear head to dissect my feelings.

Fortunately, his proximity also meant I didn't need to be there every second of the day. It was amazing the difference one extra person made in the day-to-day functioning of the Farm. Holden and Opa took turns managing the cottage or moving trees. Oma watched Orion, made cocoa for customers, and took a few turns at the cashbox as well, when Orion was napping or off with Opa.

All of that meant my proposal was actually getting finished. I'd been working on it at Pinesbury's tiny library during the limited open hours in the afternoon. A librarian from the next little town over split her time between the two locations. So, for the last four days, I'd left Orion with Oma and found a quiet spot in the seldom-visited sanctuary. Free from toddlers, and ex-best friends, and pushy wanna-be suitors.

In fact, despite the vandalism, things were finally looking up. And I was feeling better for it. There had been an outpouring of love when I'd posted about the damage and subsequent closure. People from all the nearby areas had shared messages of kindness and hope. We'd even had phone orders come through for trees, customers who just wanted to give back somehow. And there'd been a line of people waiting on the morning we'd reopened. So now I had growth in sales to include with the proposal as well.

I knew I had Holden to thank for most of it. Without him, Opa and I couldn't have finished the work so quickly. And we couldn't afford the extra touches that I knew Holden had been sneaking in, like the lights and fresh paint for the archway and signage leading to the Farm. But I wasn't ready to tell him how much we—I—appreciated it. Still, as I neared the end of my proposal, I thought about it more. Thought about how maybe we *could* be friends again. I wasn't sure my heart could risk much more though.

It was one thing to work with the challenges I was already facing, to surmount those. It was something entirely different to try to add a brand new relationship to that. If that was even what Holden wanted.

Maybe I was just getting ahead of myself. I'd always thought we were meant to be more, but maybe he realized that and that was why he ghosted me. Maybe he finally came back after all this time because he thought I would be over him by now. Moved on.

The realization made my stomach hurt and I snapped my laptop closed. Here I was getting all worked up and I didn't even know what Holden wanted. I just *assumed*. I felt the ever-familiar lump of tears wedge in my throat again. *Seriously, I know I'm sensitive to begin with, but this whole pregnancy thing is too much.* I shuffled through my bag for a tissue and pretended to blow my nose to capture an errant tear.

I'd just decided that maybe, just maybe, I could handle a friendship with Holden Moore again. But the thought that that might be *all* he wanted, sent me over the edge. Because that only meant one thing: I still wanted more. And I wouldn't be okay without that. Only... *I don't think I can trust that he'll stay.*

I tried to work for another thirty minutes before giving up entirely. My brain bought a one-way ticket to Holdenville and there was no way I'd get off the track without a more time-consuming distraction. I decided to pick up Orion and take him to the park, then to get flowers for his mother's grave. If I couldn't stop the sad memories, I'd just replace it with a different one.

On my way out the door, I pulled out my cell to check into our social media accounts. There were so many messages and comments to respond to, and I always checked our reviews as well. I'd found some great feedback and ideas there in the past.

One caught my eye as I stepped outside and I froze, staring at it. Someone had given Waldvogel Farms a one-star review because our concessions didn't include alcohol. I was flabbergasted. I didn't even know that was a thing, and even if it was, the concessions were literally brand new. A last-second addition. I just announced that. There was no time to get a liquor license.

I figured others browsing reviews would draw the same conclusion, but still. We didn't have *that* many reviews so that one really pulled down our average. Anyone just glancing over the star count wouldn't know that one of them was nonsense. They'd just compare it to the neighboring tree farm that had thousands of reviews, thus a better average, and skip us entirely.

But what could I do? If I responded it would just come across as petty. And even if I could come up with something polite and professional, they probably wouldn't change the review. It wouldn't fix anything. I was fuming when I finally took another step—and ran right into Conrad Clarke. *Shit.*

"Rosie! Hey, are you okay? I think I ask you that every time I see you," the comment could have been funny. Maybe. But it came across as entirely patronizing. I hadn't interacted much with Conrad in school, I knew he had a crush on me. And I knew Holden didn't like him. But I was starting to understand why now.

"I'm good, Conrad," I stepped away from him and forced a pleasant smile. I'd hoped to counter his comment, but instead, he took it as an invitation.

He stepped into my space again and cupped my elbow, "I've been thinking about you, babe. I was going to come check on you this week. I know you were just feeling emotional the other day." *Gross.*

"No need," I shook my arm free, "Things are great, actually. The Farm is doing really well now."

He lifted a skeptical brow.

My smile was actually genuine when I continued, "That vandalism incident actually did more help than harm. It sort of went viral. At least in the area. We've had a ton of people show up to support us. And aside from one ignorant review, which is what I was just distracted by, the feedback has been amazing."

"I see," Conrad coughed. My grin fell as I realized his expression shared none of the positivity I was feeling.

I frowned at him, "What? What's wrong?"

"Uh, nothing," he scratched his chin, "Just not sure why you're so invested in that place, babe." *Seriously*, if he didn't stop with the pet names, I'd have to slap him.

"Explain," I all but growled. Pregnancy was no joke. I didn't experience any emotion at less than a hundred percent. Still didn't give him a right to comment on it though. And right now I was a bundle of rage.

At least that was *one* hint Conrad picked up on. He took a step back again and contorted his face into a charming grin. "Well," he forced a chuckle, "I know a thing about businesses, Rosie, and a tree farm isn't a good one. I'm surprised it's lasted as long as it has. I suppose some sign of growth is good, means you'll get a better price. But I really suggest you just cut your losses. Sell. Now."

Whew, icy winter, meet volcanic summer, because I

exploded. "You know what? Fuck you, Conrad," I barely cursed in my own head, but this guy deserved it, "The Waldvogels mean everything to me. And so does that farm. I won't let it fail. We're going to make it better than ever. You'll see."

I shouldered past him and stomped away before he could respond. And I was still huffing when I picked Orion up twenty minutes later. I swore the steam coming out of my ears was melting the snow on the trees as I walked him back to the car. I saw Holden watching me go, but I didn't have the energy to deal with him right now. Not when I couldn't make up my mind.

Deciding to modify my plan only slightly, I risked needing to buy gas sooner to drive to the big park in the city. It was chaotic and busy and Ri loved it. The perfect place for me to be entirely too focused on him to think about stupid men and their know-better attitudes.

It worked, too. By the time Ri and I made it home, we were exhausted, chilled to the bone in the best way, and happy. For the first time in weeks, we both fell asleep easy.

When Orion woke up content and snuggly, I decided to take advantage. Every day was hard, but mornings were the hardest. But I'd managed to turn the day around yesterday and have a wonderful evening with my nephew. I know these moments were far too few to pass up.

So when I realized we were going to be late, I didn't care. Ri and I took a break from watching his favorite cartoon on his tablet to video chat Oma and let her know we'd be there after breakfast and not to wait up. After all, I was sure Holden would be there to annoy me. *I mean,* help her.

Orion loved the idea of video calls, but when he asked to try with his mom, my heart broke. I cuddled him closer and tried to explain why he couldn't. Not an easy topic to cover with a toddler. Ten minutes of tears later and we'd managed to get back to enjoying his show. And I had reaffirmed for myself that caring for Orion and the Farm were all my heart could handle right now.

After another hour or so of soaking in time with Ri, we decided to go to the Farm. He had started asking about truck rides with Opa and Oma's cookies, and I did have work to do. Conrad's comment was still floating around in my mind, even if I had been able to push it most of the way down. It was time to live up to my own words, though, and that meant facing the day.

For once, Ri was happy to put his jacket on and I barely had time to ensure everything we needed was packed up before he was running to the car. The whole way there he chattered about Christmas and Opa's truck and all the things he was going to do today. He even mentioned Holden and my chest squeezed.

"'Den has blue truck," I could see his grin in the rearview mirror. Orion loved trucks, so Holden had already won points there. But he didn't like strangers, and that's what Holden had been just a couple of days ago. *Too much, too soon.*

I did not park at the front of the Farm like I had the day of the vandalism. As soon as we reopened, it was so busy I didn't want to risk leaving my car there and having someone just leave because they couldn't find a spot. It made me realize I needed to include a budget for expanding the parking area in my proposal. While that tipped the costs higher, I was glad to have discovered the need early.

So I wasn't prepared when I walked onto the Farm through the side lot and heard absolute silence. No kids squealing, no boots crunching the icy snow that always accumulated closest to the trees. I deviated from the path to the house and turned toward the cottage. As I got closer, sounds of Christmas music filtered through the still air, but that was it. The Farm was empty.

"What the...?" I caught myself. I was not about to make a habit of cursing, not now with Orion in tow. But even he had picked up on the weird vibe in the air. He was peering around curiously, twisting and turning in my arms.

Even on our least busy days, there were always a few people milling around by now. They'd take a long lunch to pick out a tree and surprise their kids with it. Or it would be their chosen day off to prepare for the holidays. Something. But right now, I saw no one.

A sick feeling settled in my stomach, twisting and churning up the decaf I drank on the way here. Pulling Orion tighter against my chest, I hesitantly continued toward the cottage. My head swung from side to side, tracing any permeations into the quiet. There was nothing but the sounds of winter critters to add to the muted carols.

I found Oma first, humming out of tune while she swept up in the little office. "'Ma," Orion squealed, too excited to even attempt the first sound. I let him slide down my side, half in a daze. As soon as his little feet hit the floor, he scurried over to her.

"Little star," Oma scooped him, abandoning her broom, and planting kisses on his cheeks until his giggles filled the heavy silence. She turned to me, "It is quiet this morning, *Röschen*. Good time to clean up."

"I guess," I murmured, glancing into the front room of the cottage where the sales window was. Still no one. "It hasn't been this quiet in days, though. I would have expected business to taper off, not disappear entirely."

Oma tutted, shuffling around me toward the door, with Orion still in her arms. "We do not control these things." I watched as she stepped out and froze, "Ah, Holden! There you are."

My blood ran colder than the ambient air temperature at the sound of his name. *Not ready, not ready.*

"Oma," I heard a crunch and a pause that I assumed meant he'd stopped to talk. "Hey, Ri," butterflies and bombs took turns fluttering and exploding inside me. *He's calling him Ri.*

"*Röschen* is inside. It is very quiet, maybe she will tell you where to hang the lights now," Oma suggested. I dropped into the chair and pinched the bridge of my nose. I just knew she'd been biding her time for the opportunity to force us into conversation. The woman was too clever and meddling for her own good.

More crunching and the creaking of the door signaled Oma's departure and Holden's entrance to the room. It was already small, but it felt so much smaller now. *No surprise, with the giant elephant and all.* I didn't look up. Couldn't. But I tracked his movement through the corner of my eye.

"Uh," Holden glanced around the room then gestured at the boxes of lights before continuing, "I tried asking where to hang them. A few times. She said you didn't tell her."

I nodded, still not daring to let our eyes meet, "She never even asked."

Through my lashes, I could see him smile, "Yeah, I didn't think so. I know you're not ready yet, *Rö*—Rosie. If you can just tell me where to put them, I can get out of your space." He spoke so quietly, so slowly. Like he was testing the integrity of a frozen lake. Wondering if it would hold, or shatter apart. *Fair.*

"Um," I finally stood and took a hesitant step toward him. Unable to actually look at him when we spoke though, I dipped down and grabbed a box, "I was thinking of lighting all the trees that line the path from the entrance to here. Sort of like a guide..." I passed the box into his hands.

Our fingers brushed and I forgot to breathe for a moment. Holden did, too. I snapped my hands back to my chest. "Yeah," his voice came out raspy and rough, "That's, uh, that's a great idea."

I nodded, staring off somewhere above his right shoulder. Fiddling with the zipper on my coat. It was so warm in this freaking room.

"Consider it done," Holden's head bobbed once before he turned to leave.

"Hey," I stopped him quickly. I couldn't help myself, I needed to know what was happening. And maybe he knew. It would save me time trying to solve the problem if I didn't have to hunt it down.

"Do, uhm, do you know why it's so quiet this afternoon?" I asked.

I watched as Holden fought to hide his disappointment in my question. He'd been hoping I'd say something else, but I wasn't ready for any other conversation. He cleared his throat, "No idea. I actually just got here. Eric needed my help at the Inn this morning."

"Oh," I sighed. He paused. But when I didn't say anything more, he turned to leave again. And this time I let him.

I waited until I heard the door close quietly before I moved again. First, I needed to check in online. It didn't snow a lot last night, but maybe there had been an accident blocking the road into Pinesbury. Once I knew what was going on, I could force myself to take advantage of the downtime, like Oma had said. I needed to do a thorough accounting of sales and the insurance had emailed yesterday.

Grunting and trying to bend around baby, I hefted my bag up on the desk and pulled out my laptop first, setting it to the side. Then I rifled through until I found my phone.

"Oh, fuck! Oh, my god," I couldn't fight the curse or the

exclamation as I stared down at the screen. The room swayed around me, the ground unsteady. The icy lake had shattered and I was going under. Helplessly sinking.

I was vaguely aware of stomping noises and the sound of the door crashing open. Heavy breaths and hands gripping my arms, forcing me back into the desk chair.

"Hey, hey," Holden's voice infiltrated the haze, but I was still focused on the screen. Thousands of notifications. All angry, hate-filled comments. I swiped over to our review page. Hundreds of new reviews. *One star.*

"No. Oh, no..." my speech was limited to unintelligible sounds of despair. This couldn't be happening. *How?* How was this happening?

"*Röschen.* Hey, *Röschen,* what's wrong? Is it something with the baby?" Holden's palm gripped my cheek and for the first time in years, I looked at him. Really looked at him. And everything hurt.

It was all over. This would destroy the Farm. Everything I had spent months dedicating my life to. Years, really. Even if I hadn't intended on coming back, I still wouldn't have let the Farm fail. Then Daisy's last will called and that had been it. Orion and the Farm. That was my life. With the Farm gone, I had no idea how I was going to care for Orion now. I was barely making ends meet.

"*Röschen,* talk to me," Holden begged when I still couldn't speak.

And I was so angry. At the world. At him. He should have been here. He should have been there for me all these years. That's what friends did. Maybe I could have gotten over him, too. If he had just told me five years ago. Instead, I'd pined for him. Endlessly. Hoping, wishing, dreaming that he would come home to me. Even when I told myself I had given up, somewhere in the back of my mind, I couldn't let it go. Let him go.

Now he was just back, like nothing ever happened. But so much had happened. It happened, and it festered and bruised. It turned into an ache so deep it could never leave. And I felt it all, all over again staring down at the senseless act of cruelty. I didn't know how or why, but scrolling through the evil words, I knew it had been deliberate. Knew this was the vandals, back again when they realized their M.O. was no good anymore. But this was. *They win.*

Finally giving up, Holden tugged the phone from my trembling hand, "Oh, shit..." I stared at the screen while he scrolled. Squatted in front of me, one hand holding my phone, the other braced on my thigh, he witnessed the virtual evisceration. The comments went on and on. I hated that it was so easy to read them, even upside down. The shortest cut the deepest. And more were coming in as he was reading old ones.

I had to stop it. I snatched the phone back and made all the accounts private. It wouldn't stop anyone who had already followed the pages, but it would slow the bleeding. At least on the pages I could control. There was nothing I could do about the review pages, though.

This was the final push before Christmas. We needed the sales if we were going to make it another year. Even if I could convince the platforms this was a deliberate attack and get them to take down the reviews, I couldn't do it in time. It would take weeks we didn't have.

Holden realized it, too. I watched it hit him. His hands scrubbed over his face. The breath he exhaled was as shaky as I felt. "We'll fix this, Rosie. I promise. We'll find a way to fix this," he swore. I could hear him try to mean the words, but there was no plan there. No plan to be made that wouldn't come too late.

"Don't you get it? They won. We can't just *fix* this," at some point, I had started crying. Everything I said sounded watery. Drowned in that icy lake. Gone.

"No," his head shook hard, his beanie rising over his ears from the movement, "I don't accept that. You've worked too hard for this, *Röschen*. I know you have. We'll find a way. We'll—"

"It's over, Holden," I cried, interrupting him. Stopping the trail of delusion. The sooner he accepted it, the better. The sooner I could take Orion and move on. Far away from Pinesbury. Anger wove through my words, through every thought, but the tears wouldn't let up either. "This is unfixable! You can't repaint the freaking internet."

GODDAMMIT. Rosie's tears would forever be the one thing that could bring me to my knees. And I was. Crouched before her, I desperately wanted to stop her pain. Needed to stop it. Maybe *I* couldn't repaint the internet. But I thought I might know someone who could.

I slid the phone out of Rosie's hand and leaned past her to grab the laptop, too. I wasn't sure I needed them, but I knew she didn't. She didn't need to keep living in the nightmare. Either I could fix it, or I couldn't, but the play-by-play wouldn't help Rosie

"What are you doing?" Watery eyes turned up to look at me. Inches away. We'd never been quite this close before. I could see flecks of dark slate in her gray-blue eyes. My gaze dropped to her lips, following the salty streak of tears. Her tongue darted out to lick one away and I about died. I wanted to be the one to kiss away those tears. But now wasn't the right time.

I settled for lifting my chin and pressing my lips to her temple, "I'm going to figure out how to repaint the internet." It was a daring move, considering everything. But I needed it, and so did she. Something to cast a Christmas spell.

Her snort was the best sound I'd ever heard. She didn't believe I could, I didn't know if *I* believed I could. It made her laugh, though, and I wasn't going to complain about that at all. Not when it slowed the flow of tears. Now I just needed her to go somewhere that didn't involve the Farm.

"Take Orion to lunch, maybe ice skating in town," she started to cut me off, but I knew what she was going to say, "I got it, *Röschen,* call it one of the many Christmas gifts I missed for you guys." I wasn't sure she'd accept. My Rosie could be so damn stubborn, but I owed her and we both knew it. I hoped the reminder and the fact that it would be fun for Ri would win her over.

I watched as she chewed her lip, thinking about it. Finally, she sighed, shaking her head, "I can't go out without a phone, Holden. What if something happens?"

"Right," I looked at the device in my hand. I didn't want her to have it. And I didn't want to give her mine, either. Not because I was worried about what she would find. I didn't want her falling into the trap of looking this shit up again. Not until I knew for sure if there was a way to fix it.

"I'll just stay around here, Holden, it's okay," she whispered. But I could tell it wasn't. There would be no escaping thoughts of the Farm while she was *at* the fucking Farm.

"No, no," I hesitated, grasping for an idea that finally hit, "Wait! Opa's phone. It's a brick. He's here and doesn't need it. Take his phone and Orion and play hooky for a while." *Brilliant, thank god.* The perfect solution because the truth was I didn't want Rosie out of sight without a means of communication either. Not when roads were icy all over the area.

The look of pure hope in her eyes was enough to undo me. If I didn't get her out of here soon, I wasn't going to be able to stop myself from kissing her. Showing her exactly what I had come back for. And I couldn't do that until I'd solved the current problem. Until I'd earned my spot back in her life.

"Go, Rosie, I've got this," I rasped, barely maintaining control of myself, yet unwilling to put any more space between us.

She leaned back to press herself up out of the chair, but I held out a hand to help her. As she righted herself, one palm came to rest on her lower back, and the other cupped her belly. I would have sworn it doubled in size in the last week, but I knew that was impossible. I couldn't help but think it looked good on her. And I wished again that the circumstances were different.

"You really think you can help?" Rosie spoke up and distracted me from the spiraling thoughts that looking at her pregnant inspired in me. Her voice was still so weak, like she'd only accepted that I was trying to distract her from the situation. Not that she really thought it was possible.

But I believed in Christmas miracles because she always had. It was time to make one. "Yeah, *Röschen*, I really do." And I prayed Charlie would come through.

"Thanks," she nodded once, then slid past me toward the door. So careful to keep our bodies from touching. *At least she's talking to me.*

I waited until I heard her marching back down the path with Orion before I called. If I found out there was nothing that could be done, I didn't want it to affect the chance for Rosie to get a little peace.

My fingers tapped anxiously on the desk chair as I listened to the phone ring. And ring. And ring. Maybe it was an exaggeration, but I would have sworn Charlie waited for the last possible moment before picking up.

"Man, we didn't talk this much when were overseas," he answered laughing, but I couldn't manage it. There was too much pressure to get this right.

"I need another favor," I hesitated again. "That vandalism thing. It escalated. You said you had a pretty good tech guy..."

"Pretty good?" Charlie chucked, "Try the best. There's nothing Carter can't do. Especially when he's over-caffeinated. A little stereotypical, but he's too good to fault him for it."

I could feel him still prodding for the levity, but I'd used up all my feigned confidence on Rosie. If this didn't work, Rosie would be right. The Farm would be fucked. I'd snooped through the files while helping out the last few days. I didn't have a business or accounting degree, but even I could see that the profits were abysmal.

"Are *you* good, Holden?" I heard the concern in my friend's voice, the worry. Charlie Anderson knew me too well. Knew exactly what being here meant to me.

"No," I choked out. "I never should have left—"

"Too late for those thoughts," he cut me off, "What's going on now?" He'd given up on levity and was the cold, hard, serious soldier I knew him to be.

I cleared my throat and tried to focus. He wasn't wrong. It was too late for those thoughts. "The vandals went digital. All of the Farm's social media profiles are being spammed, and review sites, too."

Charlie hummed, "If it's a deliberate attack, it shouldn't be too difficult to get all that removed. It's usually bots. I think. Most of that's over my head, but I've picked things up here and there."

"The support after the damage had been phenomenal. Rosie went viral and everyone turned out. Today, the place is a fucking ghost town. The Farm can't afford the few weeks it would take for the sites to take down the reviews," I'd already thought of that, and I was sure Rosie had, too.

"Is it that bad?"

"Worse than I thought. Oma really glossed over things here. Rosie's trying to work a miracle, and she was fucking doing it. Until today."

I heard a sigh across the line, "And you think fixing the reviews will help?"

"It won't hurt, but leaving them up will," I thought about another thing, "Besides, if we can prove this was deliberate, we can file a police report. Sue for damages. It might mean the difference between making it another year or shutting down the farm."

"That's a good point, but a case like that could take a while to pay out," Charlie reasoned.

I agreed, "I know. But I'd like to stop the bleeding. Can your guy help?"

I heard a rough exhale and then, "I'll see what he can do. We should be able to trace the source if it is bots, but I'm not as confident about removing the posts. We've never had to have him do something like that."

I couldn't help the disappointed grunt. The increased sales from the last couple of days would help, but we couldn't go stagnant now. Even if it went back to baseline, I figured we could make it. But that wouldn't happen if the reviews stayed up.

"But," Charlie interjected, "If anyone can do it, Carter can. Give me a few hours and I'll let you know."

"Thanks, man," I murmured, "I owe you."

"Don't worry, I'll find some way to call it in," he chuckled and the line went dead.

🌲

Charlie was right. Carter was a fucking miracle worker. I got the call twenty minutes before Rosie and Orion got back to the Farm. I highly doubted whatever he had done was technically legal, but all the reviews, comments, and posts made today had been removed. He was keeping up with new posts, too, and had managed to find the origin of the posts.

Someone had posted a request for virtual sabotage on a dubious corner of the internet. Carter was still working on tracing whoever had made the post, but it was only a matter of time. We'd stopped the bleeding, and we'd have something to take to the police soon enough. Rosie was going to be so relieved.

I tried to contain my excitement as she came walking up the path, Ri perched on her hip. This wasn't over entirely. I had to believe the saboteurs would be trying something else as soon as they realized we'd stopped the virtual assault. I also wasn't sure it would be enough to get the Farm to the end of the season. It had happened and people had seen, Rosie would have to make some kind of a statement and there was no way to predict how that would go.

She looked tired as she trudged toward the house. Her cheeks were flushed pink from the cold. But Orion was chattering on happily so I guessed they had fun.

"Anything?" Rosie asked, setting Ri down to scurry inside. She didn't even try to fight the exhaustion cutting through her tone. All I wanted to do was get her off her feet. Find a place where she could sit and rest and not worry. Preferably someplace I could be with her. But she wasn't ready for that. She stood, arms crossed protectively over her stomach, all but tapping her foot waiting for my update.

So I gave it. "A friend of mine was able to help out," I reported, handing over her laptop and phone. She shifted the laptop under her arm and opened her phone to scroll while I continued, "He's doing something to stop new posts and stop the bots. It was deliberate, Rosie. He's working on figuring out who is behind it."

"Well, we already knew that," she sighed, locking her phone. "Did anyone come by at all?" She glanced toward the entrance and the little cottage that I'd just closed up for the night.

I nodded, "A few. Not as many as we'd been having, but a couple sales."

"That's good, I guess," the utter dejection in her voice made my chest feel tight. I gulped, trying to fight the urge to wrap her up. "I really appreciate this, Holden," her words came out just above a whisper as she started to shuffle past me toward the house.

"Anything for you, *Röschen*," I knew my voice had gone all raspy. Lower than it needed to be. I gave away everything I was feeling with those words, but I couldn't stop it.

She heard it, too. She stopped and blinked at me, her body still so close to mine. I watched her throat as she swallowed. I didn't know if I wanted to kiss her there, or wrap a billion scarves around it so the cold didn't touch her. After another hitched breath, she dropped her gaze and kept on, reaching for the doorknob.

I wasn't ready. I couldn't let her go. "Wait," I reached out, gently wrapping my fingers around her arm, "Can we talk?" There was so much that needed to be said. So much to explain. To apologize for.

She stared at me for a second, then nodded briefly, "After dinner."

"You're staying?" I couldn't keep the excitement out of my voice. I knew she usually had dinner here, but she hadn't been since I'd been around. Now, it sounded like she wasn't planning on leaving, and it sounded like she knew I wasn't either.

"Yeah," and I could have died for the small smile she gave me, "Ri's been pretty upset that we've been missing Oma's dinners."

"I don't blame him," I slid past her to open the door and followed her inside.

Dinner wasn't easy. It wasn't like old times. But it wasn't as painfully uncomfortable as our other interactions had been. Rosie had her guard up, and that was fair. We were getting closer, though. I even managed to squeeze a few more shy smiles out of her. It felt like winning the lottery.

After we ate, Oma pulled Ri away to the living room to work on a puzzle they'd started the day before. Opa followed behind to watch the news. Rosie and I were left in the kitchen with a fresh pot of hot cocoa simmering on the stove.

I sat at the table with my heart in my throat as I watched her pour two mugs and bring them over. She sat down, and slowly twisted her mug. Staring into it like she hoped she could find all the answers she wanted there, instead of across the table where I was gripping my own mug nervously.

A tenuous silence stretched between us. I didn't expect her to start, but I wasn't sure where I should. Just saying that I was sorry wouldn't be enough, but I didn't know how to make her understand. It didn't help that my logic had been entirely flawed.

"Why, Holden?" She finally whispered, "Why did you just forget about me? About *only* me?"

I swallowed, shaking my head, "Not for one day did I ever

forget about you, *Röschen*." I could see how she could think that, but nothing would be further from the truth.

A strand of her dark hair fell into her face. The ends lightened where she'd let highlights grow out. My fingers itched to tuck it back. But I didn't. I watched her do it instead.

She was quiet, leaving it up to me to continue. "I was young and stupid, Rosie. I got your letter. I was writing back when we went on an op. I just..." I hesitated, unsure how to put it into words. "Here, let me show you something," I decided words wouldn't do it. I stood up and pulled my shirt up, exposing the jagged red scar on the left side of my abdomen. Courtesy of a hasty field medic.

Rosie's eyes went wide and I watched tears start to well up. Her hand lifted, like she might reach out and touch it, but she brought it to her lips instead. Her throat bobbing against swells of emotion. I didn't want to make her cry, but I needed her to understand why I thought it was the right thing to do back then.

I pulled my shirt down and kept going, taking my seat again. "I was this close to dying," I held my fingers millimeters apart, "And I just thought it would be easier for you. Easier if you weren't waiting for me to die."

Her head shook and a little of her old, stubborn temper flared, "It wasn't for you to decide what was easier for me. You took away my choice, Holden."

"I know I did," I sighed, "But by the time I realized what a mistake it was, I thought it was too late. Too much time had passed. Mom's letters said you weren't even in town anymore. I thought you moved on."

Her brow raised and she took a slow sip of her cocoa. My answer to that had obviously been unbelievable. I should have known that, too, should have known she would still be there.

But, "And I didn't want to reach out and apologize only to die six months later."

Rosie's lips pursed, "So, you took the choice away again."

"Yeah." I didn't have a better answer.

"That's stupid, Holden," she huffed and I almost laughed. She wasn't wrong, but she was so caught up that she let go of everything that had been weighing her down to call me out.

I smiled at her instead, tried to infuse everything I felt, all of my apology in the expression. "I know it was, *Röschen.* It was the biggest mistake I ever made. I missed you. Every second of every day."

Her chin dropped as I finished speaking, a hand dashed up to wipe away a tear. The movement was meant to be discreet, like pushing away a stray hair, but I knew her better than that. After all this time, I still knew her better than that.

"Your last letter... You said you had something important to tell me?" I wanted her to say it. To say she wanted more. I'd hoped back then, but I hadn't been sure. But I was sure now. I saw it her in eyes when I snagged that laptop. That look was easier to read than her handwriting. Not that her handwriting was easy to read. *But that look definitely was.*

But she wouldn't do it. "It doesn't matter now," she shook her head. Crossing her arms across her chest, still hunched over her mug at the edge of the table. Her body language told me she was shutting down. Protecting herself. *From me.*

"It matters to me, *Röschen,*" I tried. My hand reached out toward her, sliding along the wooden surface, but she pretended not to notice. "Tell me. Please. I want to know, Rosie. Because I think I already do. And I want that, too." That made her head shoot up. Eyes wide again. I waited. Holding my breath.

"Not now, Holden," she finally sighed, dropping her gaze once more, "I'm not ready." It wasn't what I wanted, what I knew we both wanted, but it was an inch closer. And I couldn't blame her for needing more time.

I nodded; dared to stand, move around the table, and kiss the top of her head. She let me, then got up and called for Ri and I walked them both out to her car. Promising myself I wouldn't stop trying to win back her love.

I WOKE up with a weird mixture of feelings swirling around in my belly. Orion also woke up early, ready to go to the farm and play with his new friend, Holden. And that just added to the twists and tangles I was feeling. Like a jumble of Christmas lights, I wasn't sure how to find my way to the end. If I could, the result might be magical. But everyone knows some strands just get too far gone to save. Bulbs broken and cords stretched. I wasn't sure our mess was fixable.

Even though I had been aware of the risks, they had felt sort of distant. Unreal. Until I saw that scar. Knowing that happened so quickly made me sick. I probably would have been devastated, too, and spent the next years constantly worrying. But that didn't make it okay for him to take the choice away from me like that.

And did he want more? Had he wanted more the entire time? I thought he did. Oma thought he did. Everyone in freaking Pinesbury had thought we would end up together. But I'd still been insecure about it. Unsure if I was willing to risk our friendship if I found out he didn't feel the same.

He didn't come right out and say it, but there was something different in the way he looked at me yesterday. Something stronger, something deeper. Consuming. Had he always looked at me like that? I wasn't sure and it felt like one more thing to worry about. He was back, he said he was going to stay. What if we tried and it didn't work out and I lost him all over again?

Or was I just fooling myself and he never wanted more and still didn't?

I felt more tears stinging at the thought. *Right. Gotta get out of bed before the hormones win again.* "C'mon, Ri," I tugged his tablet away and pretended I was shutting the door on the Holden Problem when I snapped the cover on it.

I vowed to spend the day at the Farm though, and not run away again. He'd worked a freaking miracle yesterday fixing the reviews and posts, so I felt I owed him that much.

Holden wasn't at the Farm when we got there. Orion was disappointed, but I felt little flutters when Oma told me that he had called to apologize and say that Eric needed help at the Inn that morning. I realized it was because he was building new roots in Pinesbury, creating ties and investing time in bringing the town back to life. Making it better than it was before.

I really, really needed to stop by there and meet Eric. We were allies with the same goal, we needed to take advantage of that. And maybe Holden could help. I left Orion with Oma while I headed to man the cottage. Wracking my brain for ways that Pinesbury Inn and Waldvogel Farms could work together. Preferably some that were budget-friendly for both of us.

It was still quiet, but not quite as haunted as it seemed yesterday. For the most part, people understood that the posts and reviews had been a deliberate attack, but they were still wary. Some of the posts had made truly horrendous claims about me, and about the Waldvogels. The realization that we'd have to prove ourselves innocent nearly sent me over the edge, but that was the digital age.

Somehow, though, I found myself trusting that Holden would pull through. We would figure out who had been behind the attack and their motives. And hopefully, that would be enough to put the rumors to rest.

I couldn't have been any more dismayed when I saw Conrad walking the path toward me again. Why couldn't he just get the freaking hint? I wasn't interested, and the more he tried, the less likely I ever would be.

"I saw the reviews," he commented when he got near. He didn't look at me, instead, he was staring off at a tree. Examining it with a critical eye. Like it had wronged him.

"Yeah," I rubbed my stomach. It was becoming a habit whenever I felt uneasy. I swore the tiny human inside me had a better sense of intuition than I did.

He nodded absently, still strolling deliberately around the tree. I decided to ignore him and fiddled with the lights on one of the trees lining the path. After everything, Holden had still gotten them up. "It was pretty ugly for a while there, huh?" Conrad's voice sounded more distant as he moved behind another tree.

"Mhmm," all I could offer was a noncommittal hum. I knew for sure I didn't want his business anymore. His persistence had gone from overwhelming to straight creepy. I found myself wishing Holden was here to scare him off.

"How'd you do it?" I was startled when he appeared right in front of me again.

"What?" I'd stopped paying attention to him. Instead letting my mind wander to thoughts of Holden yesterday. How he'd looked at me. How it had also felt overwhelming, but so good at the same time. Not too much or not enough. *Just right.*

Conrad stepped close, looming over me, "How'd you stop the posts?"

"Oh," I shuddered, stepping back. He was definitely too much. Of all the wrong things. "It was Holden. I'm not sure how he managed it, but it was amazing." I found myself smiling. Earnestly. Warmth infused deep inside and thought that might have been how that Grinch felt when his heart grew.

"Oh?"

"Yeah," I nodded."I wasn't sure about him coming back. It wasn't easy when we stopped talking. I wasn't sure I could forgive him. But I think it's good now. That he's back, I mean," I stepped closer to the tree and tugged on a string of lights, pulling it to lay more evenly.

Conrad cleared his throat, "So, you two?"

I shrugged. "We missed out on five years, but we have forever to make up for it..." I was mostly talking to myself at that point. I just needed to say what I was feeling out loud. To taste the words and see if they were just as good in the open as they were in my head. I thought they were, and judging by the somersaults, Baby agreed. Now I just needed to figure out if Holden did, too. Or if *forever* would be best friends forever.

"Right. I guess you can always count on Pinesbury's Golden Boy to save the day, huh?" I didn't like the way he said it. I glanced over and witnessed him rush to mask a calculating look with a placid smile.

I felt my brow furrow as I watched him. Feeling like I was being stared down by a predator playing with his food. I fought the urge to look for a distraction or way out of the conversation. Somehow, looking away seemed like a bad *prey* move.

"Well, this one looks good," he waved his hand airily at a tree when I didn't answer. "Should we drum up the sale?" He flashed his meant-to-be-charming grin at me.

I didn't want his business, but it seemed like the fastest way to make him leave now. I led him back to the cottage, determined not to allow any more conversation that wasn't strictly transactional. He must have sensed my icy shift, too, and for once, decided to heed it.

Ten minutes later, I watched the back of him disappear toward the main entrance. I'd tried to get him to agree to a delivery, but he insisted on picking up the tree that evening in a truck. I wasn't sure I could handle one more interaction with the man, though, and made a mental note to let Opa or Oma take over at the end of the day.

Or Holden, I smiled at the thought.

By the early sunset, I was settling in at the kitchen table with Oma. Savory aromas from the night's dinner filled the room. The Farm would be closing soon and Opa, Ri, and Holden would all be headed in for dinner any minute.

But I couldn't wait. My stomach growled incessantly until she brought me a small plate of what she'd finished. I'd barely had a chance to eat all day. Holden had gotten caught up at the Inn later than he expected and didn't make it to the Farm until mid-afternoon. And we hadn't been incredibly busy, but customers had managed to space themselves out just enough to make it difficult to get a meal in.

Something caught her attention outside as she moved around the table, diverting her to the window instead of back to the stove. I barely noticed, too busy shoveling food in my mouth, until she gasped. I looked up right as she turned back to me, "Fire! Oh, *Röschen*, there is a fire!"

"Fire?" My stomach swooped out from underneath me while I ran to the window Oma had been looking out of. I saw

Holden running, already aware of the situation. I turned and headed for the door, but she stopped me in the entryway.

"No," she pointed at my stomach, "You must not go out there. Stay here." Wrinkled hands came to my shoulders and pushed me down onto the bench. I wanted to argue, but she was right. If I got stuck in the fray, the smoke could hurt the baby. For now, it seemed far away from the house. But I was worried about something more important than the trees, too. "Orion?" I looked up at Oma, her arms still bracketing me.

She nodded once. "Yes. I will go fetch him, Otto will need to help." She clapped her hands on my shoulders once more, then grabbed her jacket and hustled out the door.

Anxious, I moved back to the window in the kitchen to watch. We were a tree farm constantly adorned with electric lights and heaters. A fire was always a risk, and we were so far out from the fire station, so we were prepared. But we'd never needed the precautions until then. I wasn't sure they'd be enough.

Slowly though, they proved to be effective. The bright orange that had lit up the darkening sky dimmed. Replaced by the dark smoke of extinguished flames. I pulled a chair to the window and stared out into the night, my food entirely forgotten.

After what seemed like hours, but was probably no more than forty-five minutes, I saw Holden emerge from the trees, trotting toward the house. I got up to meet him at the door, nervous to find out about the extent of the damage.

He pushed inside right as I got there and shut the door behind him. I stood, shifting my weight from side to side, while he caught his breath.

"We put it out," Holden was panting, his hands braced on his knees in front of me. There were soot marks on his face marring a grim expression. A foreboding expression.

"What?" I asked, unsure if I wanted the answer.

He shook his head before righting himself, "It was deliberate, Rosie. I could smell an accelerant."

I didn't have a chance to respond before the door swung open again. "That was too much excitement for an old woman. Now, where is my little star?" Oma smelled of smoke, too, obviously having ignored the risk to herself and helped with the fire. *Wait...*

"What do you mean? Ri isn't with you?" I glanced around, alarms going off everywhere inside my brain.

She frowned at me, "Opa sent him to the house when the fire started. He said I just missed him. I helped with the hose."

I turned to look back at Holden, but he was already pushing his way back out the door calling for my nephew. I chased after him, running aimlessly out into the trees. My tired, hungry body protested with every stride. We didn't see him.

"Orion," I screeched, my head swinging frantically around. The thick scent of smoke filled the air and tangled with the cold dread I felt coursing through me. Tingling down to my fingers. "Ri!" I cried one more time, but, deep down, I knew. I knew he was gone.

Fuck. Fuck, fuck, fuck. I couldn't get any other thought to cross my mind as I caught Rosie from collapsing completely in the snow. The fire was one thing. That was bad enough, even though we'd managed to put it out fairly quickly. But Orion? I felt Rosie's whole world shatter while I held her in my arms.

I didn't wait to call in reinforcements. Within in minutes of my call, Charlie and another old Army buddy, Theo Boudreaux, and his wife, Madi, were on a company plane from DC to help with the search. I wanted to believe that he'd gotten scared and was wandering around or hiding, but the fire had been intentional. My gut told me Ri had been the real target all along.

Still, Eric was on his way to start the hunt just in case I was wrong. I wasn't ready to tell Rosie the truth of what I suspected either. It took another hour for police to show up with a swarm of volunteers. I was surprised to see Donny Hooper and Conrad among them, but I appreciated it.

Flood lights around the Farm turned the night into day as

groups set off in a grid search. At some point, Rosie's sister Lily showed up with extra clothes for Rosie. I wanted to be angry at her for all she was putting Rosie through, but it was obvious that she was as sick with worry as Rosie was. Her should-be husband, Cameron, fussed over her and fought against her helping with the hunt.

Finally, he convinced her to stay by telling her she needed to make sure Rosie and the baby were okay since Opa, Oma, and I had all forbidden her from going out, too. She was exhausted, and the terrain outside the Farm was too rough and icy for her to be out. The two sisters huddled together, taking turns crying and comforting each other, while people swarmed around. Maybe I'd have to re-evaluate my assessment of Lily, but that wasn't going to happen today.

For my part, I checked the barn and the old truck and all of Ri's favorite places to play three times before I'd convinced myself that someone had taken him. I didn't want to worry Rosie with that conclusion, though, so I told her I was walking a perimeter around the Farm so Orion would see a friendly face if he wandered back. He hated strangers and tended to run back toward the house if a customer tried to talk to him, so I figured it would be a reasonable thing for him to do if I *was* wrong. But I knew I wasn't.

Six hours later, the search had been disbanded for the night. The police had very likely drawn the same conclusion I did, but hadn't mentioned it yet. I watched from outside as headlights made their way up the hill to the farm. The faintest light sweeping in through the trees. Charlie had called when they landed at a small airfield an hour away to let me know they were en route and ready. As in, armed to the teeth.

Rosie's body had finally won and she had fallen asleep on the couch before the search ended, but now I headed back inside to wake her. As much as I wanted to let her keep resting, I knew she would be pissed if I let her sleep through this.

Even in sleep, she looked overwhelmed. Pushed to the breaking point. I sat down next to her, brushing hair from her face and quietly whispering until her eyes fluttered open. "Did you find Ri?" She pushed up to a sitting position, her words slurred and groggy.

It killed me to tell her that we hadn't. That I was only waking her up because I believed someone had taken him and my Army friends were here to help. My theory didn't seem to surprise her, but she was still crying hard in my arms when the quiet knock sounded at the door.

I faltered before I managed to break myself away from Rosie to answer the door and lead them back into the living room.

"Thanks for coming," I felt myself choke up as I took in my friends standing before me. I lowered my voice to keep from waking my grandparents. Their room was at the other end of the house, but it wasn't a big house.

"No big deal," Madi plopped onto the couch next to Rosie. "Our case has hit a stalemate. All we're missing is Gabriel getting his shit rocked by a sweet little redhead." Theo had told me he was tracking some arms dealer when I called him after Charlie. But he still dropped it all to show up at a moment's notice. It meant everything to me that the family I'd built was here to support the family I'd stupidly left behind.

"She's a suspect, baby," Theo scolded her, but it lacked any heat. His gaze softened as he looked at her and I was momentarily taken aback. He left the Army before I did, and we'd kept in touch a little, but I didn't know much about his relationship. Obviously, it was the real deal.

My eyes slid to Rosie, sitting apprehensively next to the blonde. Did she know I looked at her the same way?

"Anyway," Madi continued, ignoring her husband, "As fun as *that* is to watch, this is more important. Besides, Max is giving me live updates." She turned her phone screen to us as several new texts popped up.

Rosie's face was a mix between confusion and alarm at the woman sitting next to her, but Madi wasn't deterred. She scooted closer, unlocking her phone, presumably to share the messages.

Theo smiled, then turned and nodded toward the kitchen. "Madi will distract her while we talk," he murmured on his way through the threshold.

"Rosie's not going to like being left out," I said as we formed a circle around the small island.

Charlie shook his head. "My guess is Madi doesn't like being on distraction duty either," Theo made a face that said he was right, "But we need to talk worst-case and there's no reason to scare her more. We'll fill her in when we have a plan."

"Yeah. Okay," I sighed, bracing myself against the counter.

We spent almost thirty minutes hashing out every possible nightmare we could think of, but it all came back to Rosie and the Farm. Somebody was trying to hurt one or both of them. The rash of vandalisms had stopped when most of the businesses had shut down and the remaining seemed destined to fail. They didn't start back up again until Rosie's work here started to pay off.

I knew that meant Rosie would blame herself, but I also knew that once we found Ri, I could convince her that it wasn't true. It was bad luck and evil, and there was nothing she could have done to change that. The Inn and bar hadn't been targeted, but that might have just been a matter of time. Though we had other theories about that, too.

Theo's phone chirped and he read the message before looking up at us, "Madi says Rosie's getting antsy. I think it's time to fill her in."

Charlie nodded solemnly and led us back to the living room. Rosie had obviously been focused on the doorway because she didn't even flinch when she saw us walk in. Madi, on the other hand, kept a concerned eye on Rosie for a moment longer before turning her attention back to us.

Theo bobbed his head at his wife, then sat in a chair across the couch. She got up and sat on his lap, watching me all the way. Something in her expression made me hightail it to Rosie's side. I settled on the sofa next to her. Maybe closer than we were used to, but she needed it as much as I did. And she showed me by moving closer, until our bodies were pressed together, letting me wrap an arm around her shoulders.

"We think we know what's going on," Charlie started, sitting down on the chair next to Theo's, addressing Rosie with a calm, assured voice that I couldn't hope to match at that moment.

The day's events were wearing on me, and I couldn't get the look on Rosie's face when she realized Orion was gone out of my head. The way she collapsed in my arms. I never wanted to relive that moment again, yet I couldn't stop the replay in my mind.

"You've spent a lot of time on this Farm, it's clear the work you put in is paying off," he continued diplomatically. "After the break-in here, Holden called and asked me to start looking into the vandalisms in town."

Rosie pulled away to look up at me, but I shook my head. I'd answer all her questions after Charlie was done. Anyway, the answer was simple: I cared about what she cared about. Even when she was, understandably, pissed at me.

"We're still looking into it, but it's pretty apparent they

were deliberate attacks to force the businesses to shut down so they could be bought up. Several different companies made the purchases, but our tech guy has been able to trace most of them to the same shell company."

My brows rose at the last part, which had been news to me.

Charlie looked sheepish, "Carter told me yesterday. I hadn't had the chance to call you yet."

I tipped my head so he would continue, but Rosie spoke up first, "But the Farm never had any problems. I never heard anything about Rowe's either, and nothing about the Inn."

"Hooper isn't the type to involve the cops in anything," I answered her, "I asked him and he said he had no problems, but I wouldn't be surprised if he'd made himself off-limits somehow." I wasn't exactly sure how, but threats and bribery didn't seem out of the question.

"And the Inn went out of business on its own," Charlie resumed the narrative, "My guess is Eric bought it before one of the shell companies could get their hands on it. He paid more than he probably needed to, and business was slow. I don't think the vandals expected he would need any help running out of money."

Rosie fidgeted, "Okay. But what does any of this have to do with Ri? The Farm isn't even on Main Street like the other places."

This time, Charlie took a deep breath before answering. "It's possible that there's no connection, but I don't think that's very likely. You're making something of this place, Rosie, it's putting Pinesbury on the map. Giving it a reputation as a quaint little hometown."

"That's what it is," Rosie frowned like he just insulted her.

Charlie smiled placatingly, "That's what it *was*. Pinesbury is very likely the target of one of the developers that have been taking over small towns all over the state."

"All over the fucking country," Madi interrupted. Theo shushed her and she pinched him.

"Anyway," Charlie grinned for real this time, "You're making people care about this place, which is bad for business for a big developer. They don't want pushback. You've seen yourself what negative press can do."

Rosie nodded slowly. I squeezed her tighter, knowing the punchline was coming.

"Our theory is someone is trying to hurt the Farm to hurt you. This place is pretty isolated so it's unlikely the property is a main target right now, but you trying to make Pinesbury a destination is a problem. If the Farm goes out of business, you do, too."

"So it's my fault?" Rosie's lip trembled like I knew it would when she tried to blame herself.

"No, *Röschen*, it's the fault of whoever is doing this," I pulled her closer, pressed my lips against her head, her hair snagging against my day-old stubble. She hadn't minded when I'd done that yet and I wasn't going to stop until she told me to. Not when I knew it helped by the way she sagged into me.

She huffed disbelievingly. Just like I knew she would. I still knew her better than I knew myself. And if I'd just trusted that five years ago, maybe things would have been different. If anyone was to blame, it should have been me. But that didn't help anything either.

"They had to have taken Ri during the fire," I wanted to get on to what we were going to do about getting him back.

"You think it was a distraction?" Rosie looked up to me and I found myself fighting the urge to cup her chin and draw her close. Did she know *she* looked at *me* like that? Like I might actually be the only one who keeps her world spinning?

"Yeah," I rasped, then cleared my throat because it wasn't the time. "There were a handful of cars in the parking lot when it happened. The most likely scenario is someone posing as a customer. They probably drove out of here with everyone else when the fire took hold."

Rosie sat forward and growled, and I almost smiled. Orion may be her nephew, but she fully intended to go Mama Bear on whoever hurt him. I glanced up to see Madi grinning, quite satisfied by the sound of vengeance. I made a mental note not to get on her bad side.

"I looked over some maps and satellite footage on the plane, but some local insight would be good," Theo finally decided to speak up which I was more than ready for. His tactical insight was the entire reason I asked for him in the first place. "Are there any other roads besides the one that takes you back through Pinesbury?"

I glanced at Rosie before shaking my head, "None, unless some were put in while I was gone. There are a few other properties on the way back, and anything that might be considered a road leads to one."

Rosie nodded her agreement, but didn't speak. I felt her subtle shift deeper into my side on the couch and gave her a gentle squeeze. She didn't have a target for her anger yet, and the unending emotional high was taking a toll.

Charlie asked the next question, "Do any businesses in town have security cameras that look out onto the street?"

"Uh, yeah," I was struggling to fight my exhaustion, too, "Eric, uh, the guy who owns the Inn now, he just installed some this week, actually."

"Great," Charlie's head bobbed in satisfaction, "Can you ask him to give Carter access?" I watched as my friend's eyes assessed me, "Then get some sleep. We need you ready when we've got something."

I nodded and pulled my phone from my pocket to make the

call. I woke Eric up, but to his credit, he didn't hesitate to get the information he needed to send the footage to Carter.

Then I watched as Charlie led Theo and Madi back into the kitchen to wait before I got up and snagged the blankets and pillow that Oma had left out and piled them up on the floor next to the couch. Rosie laid back down after I did. And when I lifted my hand to rest against the side of the sofa, she took it and held on.

The call came a couple of hours later, at four in the morning. It wasn't enough sleep, but I'd had to operate on less. Rosie was less adapted, and if the circumstances had been different, I wouldn't have been able to stop myself from kissing the sleepy look off her face.

But they weren't different, and Charlie had woken us up because Carter had found something. He escorted us quietly into the kitchen, where Theo and Madi were standing by the island. A laptop was opened behind them.

I wrapped an arm around Rosie as we approached, prepared for the worst. So far, all I could make out was a shiny black car on the screen. As we got closer, more details became obvious. The street outside the Inn. The child's face in the rear window. *Orion.*

The driver's face was just as clear.

"Holden," Rosie's fingers dug into my arm, I could tell she was barely breathing, "It's Conrad. Conrad has Ri."

That fucking... A familiar swell of adrenaline surged inside me. The need to go. To act. To right the wrong. The fucker had even had the audacity to show up for the search.

I looked up and saw the same expression mirrored in my friends' faces. They didn't know who he was, but it didn't matter. Someone had fucked with family and that someone had a name now. "Conrad Clarke," I addressed Charlie. He just nodded and turned his back, pulling out his phone. I heard him talking to Carter before I looked down at Rosie, "We'll find him. We'll get him back."

Charlie stepped back to the circle, "Carter's running everything about Clarke. We'll know about every property he's attached to. Any place he might have taken Orion. We'll know where he buys his goddamn underwear by the end of this."

Rosie nodded, then shifted and crashed into my chest. It felt so good to hold her in my arms, but I couldn't enjoy it. Not the way I wanted to. Still, I looped one arm tighter around her waist and laced my hand through the hair at the back of her neck. My fingers dug into her scalp, but she didn't pull away.

I held her close. And I wasn't letting go.

"Got him," Charlie stood up three hours later. We'd moved back to the living room, sitting silently in the crowded space. My grandparents had woken up and made coffee. Rosie and I both drifted in and out of sleep sitting on the sofa. No one spoke until Charlie did. But as soon as he did, everything happened at once.

Theo and Madi were up and heading toward their rental with GPS coordinates en route to their phones. Charlie took a minute to inform us that Carter had traced all properties tied to Conrad, then hacked into street camera and satellite footage to extrapolate the most likely location. Oma had started crying and Opa was doing his best to soothe her.

"Meet you at the truck," Charlie turned to me and nodded toward my family before following Theo.

I caught Opa's eye and he bobbed his head once. The only

hint I needed that it was okay to get gone, too. To bring Orion back.

Rosie stood up and followed me to the door. "Shouldn't we call the police?" She asked quietly. She'd pulled her cardigan tight around her body, one hand resting protectively on her belly, as she watched me pull on my gloves and jacket.

"We'll call them later," I grunted, sitting roughly on the bench to put on my boots. "After we get Ri back. This is what we do, Rosie," I told her, my words harder than I intended.

Her face pinched. "Do?"

Shit. I stood up. I didn't *want* to do this anymore. I didn't need her thinking that either. "Did, *Röschen,* what I *did.* What they still do. But that doesn't mean I've forgotten. The police will handle Conrad to make sure he never does this again, but there's no one better than us to bring Orion back."

She looked up at me with watery eyes, but eventually dropped her chin sharply once. I pulled her into me and kissed her temple again quickly before stomping purposefully out the door.

I made it fifty feet before Rosie chased after me, the shoes she'd hastily pulled on crunching in the snow were my only warning before she grabbed my arm and spun me back to her. "Wait! I'm going," her breath was coming out in short puffs, perfectly visible in the chilled air.

And I could see how badly she wanted this, but I couldn't risk it. Couldn't let her risk the baby. There was too much at stake. I shook my head, "No, it's too dangerous."

"Please, Holden, I need to go," she tugged on my arm again.

"*Röschen,*" I groaned under her pleading, "We don't know what else Conrad is willing to do. If you're there, I'll worry about you and the baby. I want to be entirely focused on Orion."

She bit her lip, processing my words. I watched as she let go and cupped her stomach, slowly massaging it. I laid one hand on top of hers and squeezed. She looked down at our joined hands, then back up at me. Hope and fear warred in her eyes.

Fuck it.

I kissed her and there wasn't anything I could do to stop myself this time. It took a second, but she kissed me back just as hard. Her fingers gripped into my jacket as she held on. I tasted tears on her lips and I never wanted to let go. "Promise, *Röschen*," I finally pulled away and rested my forehead against hers, locking our gaze, "I'll bring him back."

She swallowed hard and nodded, gently so she didn't break our touch. I let my hands slide up to her face and wipe at her tears one more time before I stepped back and headed for the truck.

One more Christmas miracle.

It only took two more hours before my phone rang. But that was still two hours too many. I refused to let myself count how long Orion had been gone. I thought I would make myself sick if I did. I couldn't hit answer fast enough, "Holden?" The question came out breathless, even though I hadn't done anything other than sit at the table and stare at the screen since he left me.

"We got him, *Röschen*," he answered just as quickly. My fingers involuntarily went to my lips, where he'd kissed me. The memory felt warm and fuzzy now. *He didn't leave*, I reminded myself, *he asked you to stay*.

I couldn't fight the relieved tears. Not that I cared to anyway. If any moment deserved a good cry, it was this one. "Can I talk to him?" I asked, my voice weepy. I couldn't shake the guilt I felt knowing he had been taken to hurt me. Maybe I could have set it aside before. But not know. Not when I knew who was behind it. Not when I'd straight up told him the best way to hurt me. *Twice*.

"He's sleeping," Holden broke through my thoughts, "I think Conrad gave him something, but his vitals look good. We're heading straight back to the Farm." *Freaking Conrad*. I'd never wanted to inflict harm on another person before, but now I was struggling to fight the urge.

My shaking hands twisted in the hem of my shirt, "You sure he doesn't need a hospital?" *Focus on Ri.*

I heard Holden hesitate, "The Farm is on the way. When we get there, if you think he needs it, we'll go. If not, I think it would be less scary for him to wake up at home."

Home. He called the Farm home. Butterflies took flight in my stomach, giving me something good to focus on. Some silver lining to this whole mess. "Okay," I whispered. The swell of emotion inside me was too much to feel, let alone put into words.

But Holden heard it. "We'll be home soon, *Röschen*," his voice lowered with promise.

Madi stomped through the door first, sending clumps of snow scattering around the rug. She started talking immediately, before I'd even really got the door open. "He wasn't even there," her eyes rolled, "I mean, Orion was. Clarke wasn't. Seriously, what was he thinking leaving a two-year-old all alone? When I get my hands on him..." She let the threat linger while she pulled off her gloves and tossed them on the bench by the door.

She was a little brusque, but I couldn't say I blamed her. I would have been lying if I said I hadn't thought about several ways I'd maim Conrad if I was given the chance.

"Wh—" I started asking the question, but before I could finish, Holden was walking through the door. A sleeping Orion cradled in his arms. "Ri," I sobbed, pulling my nephew away. He didn't stir, but I could feel the steady rise and fall of his chest against mine.

Holden tugged us into him, wrapping us up in his safety. I

felt his chin rubbing on my head, but my eyes pinched closed. Too overwhelmed to do anything but soak in his warmth. Shuffling around me told me the others were coming in the door and stripping off their winter gear, but I didn't care. I never wanted to move.

We did, though, eventually. Oma wanted her honorary great-grandson, too. She tugged the sleeping toddler out of my arms for her own moment of relief before Opa toted him back to the toddler bed in her sewing room. Oma following behind to tuck him in.

The whole time, Holden didn't let me go. His grip tightened when we were left alone in the chilly entryway. I felt his kisses peppering the top of my head. When I lifted my chin to look at him, our eyes locked and a flood of emotion traveled between us. So many things we hadn't said, so many things we still would. And some things we didn't need to say at all.

This time, when he kissed me, it wasn't rushed. My stomach danced while our tongues tangled. Holden's fingers twisted in my hair and I accidentally shoved his beanie off his head when I laced mine behind his neck. For a moment, our smiles pressed together, then he deepened the kiss again.

It was everything, and more than, I'd ever wanted. Five years late, but it didn't matter. He was here now. I didn't think we'd ever stop, but the sound of pots and pans from the kitchen finally pulled us apart. Again, Holden's hand drew up to my chin, his thumb erasing tear tracks, while his forehead tilted against mine.

"We'll finish this later?" He whispered and I felt giddy while I nodded back. "We need to talk, too," he added a little more seriously.

Nerves swelled inside of me and I must have sucked my lip between my teeth because he tugged it free. It wasn't that I thought we didn't need to talk, I just wasn't sure I could handle it. The past two weeks had been the most overwhelming of my life. Even more than the first two weeks I'd had Orion. Hashing out my complicated feelings about what happened between us then and what was happening now felt like a herculean task.

Holden must have sensed my trepidation, though. Because while he didn't say anything more, he did kiss me again. This one much softer, more patient and understanding. We needed to talk, but some things could be left unsaid.

"There you are," Oma's smile was knowing as we walked into the kitchen and my cheeks heated up with the thought that she may have been a little extra noisy with the pans on purpose. "*Bärchen,* your friends were just telling us the story of how my little star was rescued."

I never understood why she used the German diminutives for Holden and I, but not Orion, but I decided it still wasn't the right time to ask. The truth was, I wanted to know what happened, too. Besides Madi mentioning that Conrad hadn't been there, I had no idea how they'd gotten Ri home.

"It was very... Anti-climatic," the blonde groaned, plopping down at the kitchen table. "Thanks, Mrs. Waldvogel," she directed her next comment at Oma who had brought her a cup of cocoa.

"Baby, you say that like it's a bad thing," Theo stood behind her and accepted another mug with a silent nod of thanks.

"It's not *bad,*" she drew out the word, "Just boring." Theo scrubbed a hand over his face in what looked like exasperation and shook his head.

"I would think boring is good," Oma pursed her lips in disapproval.

Holden's hand on my lower back edged me toward the table where he sat down then pulled me into his lap. My ears instantly got a thousand degrees warmer and I wiggled a little to get free, but he held me in place. No one paid us any mind.

Charlie was laughing when he accepted his own fresh pour of cocoa. "Boring *is* good, Mrs. Waldvogel. Thank you," he took a sip before resting back in the chair. "Our team had the right property, but we think Clarke saw us coming. We noticed some cleverly disguised security cameras on the way back. Satellite imagery shows a back road leading to the house. It was overgrown at the time the picture was taken, but he must have cleared it. Orion was sleeping on an old sofa. There was no clear evidence that he had a plan for what happened next. Most likely, he realized it would be difficult to escape with a child and decided to cut his losses."

"So he just gets away with it?" I asked, somewhat distracted and still trying to get comfortable with the idea that I was sitting on Holden. Oma brought us both mugs as well and winked when she slid mine to me, before taking her own seat. Part of me was mortified, but it also felt good. Like Holden was making this statement of proof that he wouldn't leave again, with everyone here as witness.

"No," Holden's answer rumbled in his chest pressed against my back and I shivered. "Charlie's dad passed on all the information the police need to arrest him. He's their problem now."

"Unless they don't catch him soon," Madi cut in. "Then he's our problem again, but I can promise that would be the last time he causes an issue." Her expression was hard and a little menacing. I slouched deeper into Holden's arms.

"Baby," Theo warned her with a pinch on her shoulder.

"What?" She twisted to look up at him. "I'm not going to kill him," Theo choked on his cocoa when she said that. She smiled serenely and turned back to us, "Just hurt him really, really, really bad. I don't like people who fuck with kids."

Opa chuckled first from where he stood behind Oma much like Theo stood behind Madi, "It is not elegant, but it is also not wrong."

"Thank you," Madi clapped her palms on the table dramatically while Theo rolled his eyes above her. But the way his hands massaged her shoulders and she leaned back into him told me they cared deeply about each other, despite their antagonizing.

I tilted my head, watching them, until Holden caught me and squeezed my thigh. I flushed again and tried to refocus on the conversation. We lingered for a while, talking a little more about Conrad and Orion, then whatever stories came to mind. Until we'd almost forgotten the whole ordeal. Holden let me get up a couple of times to check on my nephew, but always tugged me right back into his lap when I returned.

Minutes turned to hours sitting around the table. Finally, a tell-tale cough from the back of the house indicated Ri was waking up. Holden's friends excused themselves, promising to stay in town for a few days, and left to see if Pinesbury Inn could accommodate them, too.

The house felt significantly more quiet without them in it, but I was so focused on Orion that I barely noticed. He woke up frightened about the fire, but at least he didn't seem to remember the kidnapping. We decided the best thing to do was cuddle on the couch watching his favorite cartoons and eating Oma's cookies. And Holden was by our side the whole time.

holden

THE NEXT COUPLE of days saw a huge local turnout. Well, huge by Pinesbury standards. Donny Hooper didn't bother to show up, but his daughter did. And so did Old Man Metzger. I told Rosie about what I had witnessed between Hooper and his daughter and she decided she should be the one to check in on Becca.

When I told her I wasn't trying to add more to her plate, she told me that I should just take some of the Farm chores off it for her. I laughed and agreed to the compromise. Offering to share the workload meant she was okay with me sticking around.

We hadn't had the chance to talk yet, and while she let me hold her in quiet moments and sneak in a few more kisses, I still wasn't entirely sure where we stood. I knew what I wanted, and I knew she wanted the same thing. But just because she wanted us didn't mean she was *ready* for us.

I had a plan though, or I was working on one. It meant giving away a few more markers, but it would be worth it. I just needed Eric to come through and Rosie to agree. I wasn't worried about the former, but the latter could take some work.

"I'm afraid the old truck may be lost. The insurance will not be enough," I walked up right as Opa, Rosie, and Metzger were discussing the the fate of the Waldvogel truck. It had been among the trees when the fire started, Opa had been loading it up with deliveries. It didn't go up in flames, but it didn't escape a grim fate either.

Rosie looked so sad staring at the truck. I knew it was one of her favorite features. We could replace it, but we wouldn't be able to get something so old and photogenic for a while. I took a chance and tucked her into my side. I learned it was always a little bit of a risk around other people, but it was worth it when she let me. She did now, but I hated that it was because she was so upset.

Metzger strolled around the truck, tapping on it here and there. I was pretty sure that did nothing, but who was I to interrupt the man's methods? His technique was older than I was. "No, they sure won't. But it ain't lost," he finally grunted. "I'll have it running by Spring." He paused a moment, then nodded his head like the decision was long since made.

But Rosie shook hers, "We can't ask that. It's too much."

"Pfft," he snapped the keys out of Opa's hands. Apparently, he had run through his quota of words. He turned his back on us and waved over his shoulder on his way to his tow truck.

"Holden," Rosie turned to me, the silent protest on her lips.

But I wouldn't hear it, "They do it for you, *Röschen*. You're the only one who hasn't given up on this town."

"That's not true," her head shook defiantly.

"Yes, it is," Opa's thick German accent made the words sound rough and hard, but he was gentle as he patted her cheek and headed back toward the burned trees we still needed to drag out.

I twisted her into my chest, tucking my chin down by her ear. "Be proud of yourself, Rosie. Everyone else is proud of you."

Her arms wrapped around my waist and held on. Forty-five

minutes later, we watched the old red truck disappear down the hill.

Eric called with an update toward the end of the day. Everything was ready for my plan, all that was left was getting Rosie to agree.

"Hey," I found her in the sales cottage, doing something with a spreadsheet on her computer.

She glanced over her shoulder at me, then turned back to the screen. "Hi," she sounded distracted. She tapped a few keys, then chewed her thumb, apparently analyzing whatever information it had given her.

I strolled up behind her and dug my fingers into her shoulders. She was tense and tired. Of all the times she needed to agree to my plan, tonight would be it. But I also knew it would be a challenge to get her to break away.

She groaned, tipping back in the chair, when I found a knot and used both hands to knead into it. Her chin dropped a second later as she let me continue to work at the gnarled muscle. She let out a deep sigh when it loosened and I bent over to whisper in her ear, "Have dinner with me tonight."

I was still massaging the knot, so when she whimpered, "Holden," I almost lost it. *Fuck,* I wanted every part of her and that meant more than just my hands on her shoulders making her breathy. But I had to focus on just getting her to dinner with me first. Then we could talk about going all in.

I gritted my teeth against the growing strain and hoped she didn't hear it. "You deserve a break, Rosie. Orion can stay with Oma. Just you and me, no pressure."

I didn't have to see her face to know she rolled her eyes. I could feel it, the way it rolled through her body, too.

I stood straight again and laughed. "Mostly no pressure," I moved around the desk and leaned against it so I could see her face, "I guess if you wanted, you could have dinner without me. You really do deserve some time."

Her lips twisted as she considered it. "I just don't want to be far from Ri right now. The city's such a drive and I just..." She didn't have to finish her sentence. I understood where she was coming from and already planned for that. Since she'd mentioned it, it gave me hope that she would agree.

"We're not going to the city," I smirked, crossing my arms over my chest. I was playing it a little more flirtatious but I couldn't help it.

Her brow rose, "Where could we possibly go nearby? Are you kicking your grandparents out of the house?"

"No," I smiled. I was going to tell her, but surprising her seemed like more fun now, "Come with me and I'll show you."

And fuck if I didn't love the grin she tossed back.

It wasn't anything fancy, coming right from the Farm. Neither of us bothered to change, but it didn't matter. The only thing I cared about was having some time alone with her. And Eric had kicked himself, Charlie, Madi, and Theo out for the evening so I could. As far as I knew, they'd gone to some bar in the city.

The favors I owe... Worth every single one of them, though. While we'd been working at the Farm, Eric had transformed the small Inn bar into a romantic dining room. Sure, the wallpaper was half-stripped still and there was definitely a good bit of dust floating in the air. But it was quiet and private, and he'd set up a table in the middle of the room and drove all the way to the city and back to bring food from what he claimed was the best Italian place in a hundred miles in any direction. Wine was obviously out of the question, but Oma made homemade cider for us instead.

"You decorated," Rosie commented as we stepped inside the dimly lit room. She shed her coat and beanie and I tossed hers, and mine, onto the bar top.

"Well, Eric did," I smirked as I pulled out her seat for her. He did a great job, too. More than he said he was going to. I hadn't seen it before we got here. He'd strung Christmas lights around the room and set the table with some kind of holiday greenery. A small tree, Waldvogel, no doubt, was lit and decorated in the corner of the room. "Be right back, food's in the kitchen."

She hummed an acknowledgment as I hustled out of the room. Maybe I could have given her a tour and picked up the food on the way, but I hadn't thought about that. So now I was practically running, half nervous she'd leave if I left her alone too long.

I tried to pretend I wasn't huffing when I came back into the room. "I told him you were a Hallmark fan," I grinned as I settled the food on the table and took my seat. Rosie's lips tipped up into a sad smile that froze me, plate in mid-air. "What's wrong?"

"Uhm, nothing," her chin dipped and she stared at her hands in her lap. "I just haven't watched those in a long time."

Shit. I could guess whose fault that was. "Well," I gulped, "Maybe you could start again. Maybe we both could."

"Yeah, maybe," she breathed, her smile lifted ever so slightly to something a little more hopeful. I could work with hopeful.

It didn't take long before the awkwardness subsided and we fell into conversation that had always been so easy for us. Hearing her laugh again was long-missed music to my ears. That was my own fault, too, but I tried to push down those thoughts and focus on these new moments with her.

After we ate, I led Rosie on a tour through the Inn. I even showed her the water heater I helped move and rooms I'd never been in. Anything to keep the night going. But the more I showed her, the quieter she got and I felt my nerves starting to fray.

By the time we'd made it to the last wing, she'd gone totally silent and I was chatting incessantly to break the tense air. She stopped abruptly in the middle of the hall, "I was going to tell you that I loved you."

"What?" I spun around and froze as her words hit me.

She swallowed hard and looked down at her hands, "That last letter. What I wanted to talk to you about. I was going to tell you that I loved you."

"Oh," my heart started beating again. Much faster this time. *Was that what she was thinking about while she'd been so quiet?* I approached her slowly, then tipped her chin up to look at me, "I know." Maybe it was a little overconfident, but she'd said it out loud. Finally. The words I'd spent five years hoping I'd get to hear her say.

But Rosie thought I had misunderstood her. "No, I mean... As more..." she hesitated and chewed her lip. I watched her find enough confidence to blurt out, "That I *love*, loved you."

I smiled at her, "I know."

"What?" She looked up at me surprised, even though I had already told her that I thought I had figured it out. That if I was right, I felt the same way. Maybe I hadn't been as obvious as I thought.

"I know, Rosie," I tucked her hair back, unable to stop myself from touching her. I'd waited too long for this. "At first, when I read it, I thought you met someone and you wanted to break it to me easy. But you wouldn't have done that. You spent an entire double-sided notebook sheet describing that professor you hated."

"So?" Her eyes searched mine and it killed me that we'd come this far and weren't there yet. She didn't trust herself that she knew me better than anyone else.

"I can name everyone you met that first semester," I told her.

She frowned, her nose wrinkled up, "I don't think I could do that anymore."

I couldn't fight my smile looking down on her, "I spent the last five years memorizing those letters, *Röschen*. Every single one."

"I..." Her head shook with my admission. Then realization dawned, "But you knew? How I felt? The whole time?" She pushed herself out of my arms and I knew she was struggling to reconcile what I was telling her. To understand why it took five years, but I didn't have a good answer for her.

I scrubbed my hand over my face, knowing my logic was flawed. Knowing that she wouldn't be able to understand because I made the wrong choice. Finally, I nodded. I had to tell her, and I had to hope she would forgive me. "I realized, pretty quickly. And it scared me to death because I didn't know if I'd be alive to tell you that I loved you, too."

It was a risk, but I stepped close again. In her space. She let me.

"Or worse," I continued, lowering my voice, "That I'd get to hear you say those words. That I'd get to say them back." I captured her face in my palm and slowly slid my fingers back behind her neck, tilting her chin to look up at me, "But that I wouldn't make it out of that goddamn desert to kiss you." My lips brushed hers with my last words and when she didn't pull away, I deepened the touch.

And for a full minute, she kissed me back. Then she finally eased back and looked up at me. I sent up a silent thanks that she didn't try to extricate herself from my arms again. "When you told me the other day, I... I thought you just meant our friendship, I didn't realize you meant that you were afraid of losing more."

Yes. There it was. Her fingers tangled in the fabric of my shirt, every brushing touch told me we were figuring this out. *Finally.* "I tried to tell you," I *had* asked her to tell me what she was going to say. And that's what she'd started this conversation with, anyway. I smirked at her.

I watched her eyes roll, "You tried to get me to tell you first."

"I wanted you to remember how you felt before I told you just how badly I fucked up," I knew my grin went lopsided and I wasn't being entirely serious. Part of me had just been worried she didn't still feel that way. I didn't want to scare her by saying it first.

"Holden," her palms came to my chest in a gentle shove, but it wasn't enough to separate us. She picked up that I was teasing her. Just a little. I told her everything. I told her that I'd known all along, had wanted the same thing, but fucked up and thought it was better to ignore it. And she still kissed me. She was still here in my arms. So, what if I was too thrilled to be so serious anymore?

I snugged her tight again, flushed our bodies together, and relished the feel of her against me. I wasn't worried about scaring her now, "I love you, *Röschen*. And I kind of hoped you still loved me, too."

"Past tense?" Her fingers traced up my chest, pressing deeply into the muscle and rippling the fabric of my t-shirt along their path. The tilt of her lips told me she was teasing, too, but her teasing was much, much worse.

"Past and present," my voice had gone hoarse. Her touch sending electrical sparks all through my system, lighting me up like a fucking Christmas tree. "All these years, I hoped you would still love me when I came home. And I hope now that I'm not too late."

"You're not too late," she breathed. This time, it was her lips that brushed mine.

She'd been my teenage crush and I had wanted her then. But now she was all woman, and I couldn't not have her.

Soon.

THIS TIME, *I* kissed *him* first. Thoroughly. And everything in the world felt righted again. And maybe I should have been more upset. He'd known how I felt about him all that time and hadn't done anything. Worse, he'd acted deliberately against us.

But he'd also felt the same way about me. For that entire time. As much as I suffered losing my friend, and the person I wanted to spend my life with, he suffered just as much. More, maybe, because he knew what I didn't.

I was angry that he'd taken the choice away from me, but I was happier that he was here now. And the good he'd done in the last couple of weeks had shown how deeply he regretted that choice. Besides, I was proud of him. Proud of what he'd left to do and the man it made him.

I wouldn't have wanted to be a reason he didn't reach the goal he'd set for himself, and maybe I would have been. Or maybe I would have lost him. There were so many maybes, so many things that could have gone differently. But the past was the past and we couldn't change it.

A million maybes, yet he was still standing here right in

front of me. Hands in my hair, lips locked on mine. *A million maybes, but we still made it.* Excitement and anticipation swirled inside me. Spiraling from my head down to my toes, stopping to linger where his hips were pressed into mine.

I wanted him. Now, forever. In every way.

Now I just had to figure out how to tell him.

Years ago, when I pictured our first time, I didn't think I'd be pregnant already or have a curfew looming in the back of my mind. Not that the curfew was all that legitimate, but I wasn't ready for Orion to be waking up without me. We didn't have to rush, either. I just... Didn't want to wait.

We'd already waited five years.

"I should get you back to Ri," Holden pulled away, dumping cold water on my thoughts.

"It's okay," I stumbled over my words as he escorted me back down the hallway. I wasn't ready to go, but I wasn't sure how to say what I wanted either.

How exactly would one say they want their best friend to take them back to their hotel room and ravish them? I couldn't even *think* it without blushing and feeling all flustered.

"Hey, look," the answer caught my eye, hanging there in the middle of the corridor, "Mistletoe!"

Holden froze, staring at the offending plant, then his head turned to me, then it turned to the door it was hanging right outside of. "Eric," he grumbled, although he tried to keep it to himself.

"Wouldn't it be a major holiday faux pas to ignore it?" I tugged his hand until I pulled us both underneath it.

"*Röschen*," he grimaced, his head tipping back, "Eric's an asshole. He put that right outside my room."

Now or never. I summoned up all my courage, "Or maybe he just knew you'd be too much of a gentleman." *Alright*, not exactly an outright seduction. But I was doing my best.

Holden stared down at me and I knew I was right. There was a war going on in those chocolate eyes. "I want you, Rosie. Fuck. More than anything, I want you. But I know I sprung a lot on you tonight. Not just tonight. We can wait if you want."

Nope. "I actually don't want that at all," I pulled him by the shirt until his body slammed into mine again. *Much better.*

"Fuck," he groaned. And then his mouth was on mine and I wasn't sure if I was breathing, but that was okay. *Who needs to breathe?*

Not me. Not when he was lifting me up and leveraging my back against the door to his room. Was it crazy if I almost hoped this old Inn was so dilapidated that it would crumble under our weight? Right now, it was just another barrier between everything we'd been building up.

Holden's warmth pressed against every inch of my body as I wrapped my legs around his waist. Pulling him tighter, closer. Right....*there.*

I wasn't breathing, I was *whimpering* when I felt the hard length of him pushing up against my pelvis. My leggings doing nothing to ease the intense pressure. *Thank god.* They were another barrier, but at least not a very good one. I ground my pelvis into his, seeking the friction only his body could give right now.

"Holden," and maybe I was begging, but I didn't care, "I need to feel you. All of you."

"You'll be the death of me," I felt the gritty words on the base of my neck. It wafted over the skin where the trail of kisses he left was still tingling, sending shockwaves right to my core. *More,* I wanted more.

"Mmm," I hummed, tugging on the back of his t-shirt. It wasn't coming off with my legs wrapped around him. No matter how desperately I yanked. "Please don't. I just got you back."

"Guess you'll just have to let me take it slow then," he taunted me and I *ached*. I didn't know if I'd ever been so sensitive before. So desperately needy. If he stopped right now... Well, I couldn't think clearly enough to know what I would do. Probably just combust.

I shook my head. My hands tried to find a grip on his hair, but it was too short now. I huffed, unable to do anything more to express my dissatisfaction.

"Promise, Rosie," the gravel in his words was already undoing me, "You won't mind." He wasn't stopping his plundering hands, though, so I quit arguing. But I did grip his neck and yank his mouth back to mine. I'd let my fantasies run this far, but this was so much better already. The taste of his lips on mine was so much sweeter. His tongue stroking mine was so much more overwhelming.

My eyes were closed, but if I opened them, I thought I would have been blinded. My senses were too overburdened by everywhere his body touched mine. I wouldn't be able to process any more input.

I felt self-conscious when his palm tucked under my shirt and brushed over the swell of my belly, but he didn't seem to mind it. "We'll have a couple of these, right?" His fingers dug in, massaged, and then slid slowly up to my breasts to continue his ministrations. "Fuck," he breathed the curse into my mouth, "I can't wait."

"Y-yeah," leave it to Holden to feel my insecurity, turn it on its head, and make it erotic. My hips rocked against him of their own will. Seeking, needing.

He let go with one hand and I was vaguely aware that he was fumbling with the door. The sound of a key scraping and missing repeatedly snuck in between the sounds of our pants and moans. "Goddammit," he murmured, ripping his mouth from mine to pay attention to what he was doing.

I couldn't be deterred though. I dipped my chin into his neck, sucking kisses like he'd done to me. He ground into me even while still trying to unlock the door with his wrong hand. Finally, there was a faint *click*. Then the door was slamming open and bouncing off the wall. He didn't stop to close it.

We were alone here. We couldn't be bothered to care.

Holden fell into the bed, still holding me, pinning me underneath him. His lips found mine again. Hungrily devouring me. In the new position, I was able to loosen my hold around his waist and finally start working his shirt over his body.

I was clumsy about it though, so he leaned back and tugged it off himself. When he bent back over me, his kiss was gentle. Still just as eager, but less greedy. His hands threaded through my hair, tilting my face until it was just right for him to deepen the kiss again. But it was still slower, still as unhurried as unrelenting.

I melted under his touch. My fingers followed the lines of hard muscle on his back and shoulders, up to cup his chin and then down his chest. His skin was so hot, I felt welded to him. Carefully, he pushed up on my shirt again. Sliding up, up, until he had to pull it over my head.

Only then did he really pull away, sitting back to look down at my body. The thin bralette I wore did nothing to hide the push of my nipples against the fabric. He was reverent, the way his gaze mapped out every inch of me. He slid his hands over my skin, from my hips, up to my bralette until he slowly tugged that over my head, too.

Then he bent over to suck a nipple into his mouth, lavishing it with gentle strokes, while he pinched and rolled the other between his fingers. My moans echoed in the nearly empty room. I rolled my hips up, looking for his. Hunting that friction again. But he eased up, away from their reach, and swapped sides. Attending to my other breast with just as much concentration.

"Holden," I was begging again, but it wasn't enough. I needed him. Now. My body burned for his.

"Trust me," he murmured against the skin of my throat, then let his mouth blaze a trail down my abdomen. His body slid off the edge of the bed as he went. As his feet hit the ground, he tucked his fingers under the waistband of my leggings and pulled them down, taking my panties with them. He had to stop to pull off my boots first before he could get the black cotton and lace all the way off.

The way he looked at me, I'd never felt sexier. Being sexy had never been something I was good at, anyway. Not up until that moment when it looked like he might eat me alive. My thighs tipped open in brash invitation. He groaned, deep and jagged, as his thumb traced over me, spreading wetness across my skin. I didn't think I'd ever been more aroused. More longing and ready. And my body made sure he knew it.

Holden laid back down on the bed, next to me this time, then tugged me on top of him. I started to scooch down to kiss him again, but his hands on my ass kept me from moving any lower. I glanced down at him between my legs, only to see a devilish grin looking back up at me.

"Headboard, Rosie," he ordered, his palms sliding around to my hips. I was confused, until he tugged me down, his tongue plunging inside me mercilessly. There was no teasing; no lead-up or warning. He was just there. Everywhere.

"Oh," *oh*. The headboard was a necessity. It was all I could do to hang on while he lavished and explored every inch of me. His fingers traced gently over my skin, in direct contrast to what he was doing with his mouth. A gentle caress by a ravenous man.

I saw stars. His tongue dipped and swirled. Nipping at my

clit, sucking. Doing things I'd never felt before, never even imagined were possible. All the while, tenderly, *lovingly,* drawing shapes over my skin with the faintest touch of his hands. *Ruined.* I was gone for him, just like I always knew I would be.

Tension coiled tighter in my belly. Twisting, tangling. Sparkling like tinsel on a tree. I was going to... One palm came down on my ass and I *screamed.* In the back of my mind, I registered that I was thankful we had the building to ourselves. But, mostly, I was too far gone to be embarrassed. He never let up. Not while my body writhed above him. Not when I ground down so hard I thought he would suffocate. Not when the convulsing shudders of my orgasm caused me to spill to the side.

No, Holden's tongue followed me all the way down. Riding out every wave, seeking more and more until my body had no more to give. Only then did he let up, and he did it so gently. Trailing kisses at the crease of my thigh, around and up my belly. Across my sternum and up the column of my neck. Slow, lingering, invigorating kisses that started the swell of need inside me again.

He leaned away from me just long enough to strip his jeans from his legs, then pulled me back on top of him. This time, our bodies aligned and I felt the head of his erection nudging at me. Demanding to be let in.

"I know you're already..." he hesitated, his palms cupping my small bump, "But I'm clean. I mean... I wanted to ask..."

"Yes," I stopped him. I wanted all of him, even if I hadn't already been pregnant. It wasn't like it had happened the usual way, anyway. And I'd known my whole life that he would be it for me.

"*Fuck,*" he gripped the back of my neck and pulled my lips to his as he plunged inside me, splitting me in half. His hold didn't loosen, so I ended up moaning my pleasure deep into his mouth. He swallowed my cries with his next breath.

Slowly, his hips rolled under me. Pulling back, then thrusting deep inside again. My ears felt hot as my body warmed to the welcome invasion. I bracketed my arms around his head and my hair fell, enveloping us. Trapping our hungry pants.

"Heaven," he whispered, "Fuck, Rosie, this is heaven. I told you you'd be the death of me." He was rambling, muttering praise between curses and groans. His words adding to the tension I felt building inside me.

Holden's hands gripped my hips and helped me set the pace. Rocking, grinding, and bouncing against him. With every move, I felt myself rising higher and higher. Looking for that peak so I could once again tumble over in bliss.

The sounds I was making, they were primal. So starved for everything he was giving me. Every ounce of friction against my over-sensitized skin. Right when I thought I couldn't take it anymore, couldn't last a second longer, he flipped me over.

My back hit the bed, the soft blanket on my heated body was too much. I thought I would burst into flames when he sunk back into me. My legs wrapped around him automatically, pulling him closer again. I tried to do the same with my arms, looping them around his neck, but he wouldn't let me pull him in any closer than where our noses touched.

"Rosie," he breathed over me, "Look at me. Let me see you."

When I opened my eyes, warmth flooded me. I felt tears well up and threaten to spill over. He didn't stop, though. Didn't stop moving and thrusting inside me, slowing to grind against my clit every few strokes. When the tears did finally escape, he wiped them away, one at a time with his thumbs.

But he never, ever relented. Never broke the stare that said everything we hadn't found the words to say yet. The deep complexities of emotion that words may not ever have been able to capture. We said them with our bodies, with our touch.

And when I exploded this time, I felt him come with me. Distantly, like I was floating in space. I kept going, even when he was done, and he brought me back to earth slowly, with rolling thrusts and soft kisses along my cheeks and jaw. Words of love and adoration trickled in between them.

When I fully landed, he tipped to the side, landing next to me in the bed and pulling me against his chest. His arms snaked around me and I tucked my chin into the crook of his neck, feeling my heated breaths waft back at me. Gentle fingers caressed my spine, skimming along with the lightest touch.

It wasn't long before I felt myself slipping under, exhaustion and warmth pulling me toward sleep that I desperately wanted, but couldn't have. "I need to get back to Ri before he wakes up," I murmured. I didn't *want* to leave, but I also wasn't sure I could stay. I didn't just make decisions for myself anymore.

I felt him nod against me, "I know, *Röschen*. Just let me hold you a little longer." I couldn't fault that. I *wanted* that. I wanted to spend forever in his arms.

"Holden?" I whispered into his skin, realizing what I'd forgotten to say in the hall.

"Hmm?" He hummed into my hair, snuggling me tighter.

I wriggled back so I could look at him, "I love you, too."

"Cops found Conrad. He was pulled over trying to cross the border into Canada," Charlie strolled up to us standing by the sales cottage. We'd spent all day finishing up the cleanup. I was grateful to have Holden's friends still here to help because customers had started trickling back in for last-minute purchases.

Fortunately, the insurance would pay for the lost trees, but it was still going to be tight. I wanted to make sure we made the best impression for the crunch-time shoppers so they'd come back next year, too.

"Oh, and I'm pretty sure my dad wants to buy all of your trees," Charlie smirked. And absolutely dumbfounded me.

I swore my eyes bulged, "Wh-what?"

"Well, maybe not all of them," he looked around, "But probably most. Everyone at Anderson Security is getting a Waldvogel tree this year. He's sending a truck to pick them up tomorrow."

"Oh, my god," I was grateful when Holden slipped an arm around me before I completely collapsed. I wasn't sure exactly how big of a company his father owned, but if it was going to be *most* of our trees, it was no small thing.

We'd be set for next year. Completely. And, with the business loan, we'd be able to start introducing the new features sooner, maybe even by summer. It was more than I could have ever hoped or dreamed of nine months ago when I found myself back in Pinesbury permanently.

A year ago, saving Pinesbury hadn't even been on my radar. Now, with Holden by my side, it seemed like kismet. A certainty.

"Thanks, man," Holden reached out and shook Charlie's hand, who responded by tugging us both into a hug.

"Anything for family," he murmured between our heads. He pulled back and patted Holden's shoulder, "You sure you don't want that spot on Bravo though? I'd love to have you."

My heart dropped. Was that what Holden wanted? Was I holding him back? What if he decided to leave again when he realized it? I thought I'd worked through all of these feelings last night, but apparently, I hadn't.

"Nah," Holden squeezed me before I fell completely down

the rabbit hole, "It took me five years to find my way back to Pinesbury. There's no way I'm leaving now."

"Fair enough," Charlie chuckled. His head bobbed as we heard footsteps. Holden let go of me to look over his shoulder at the incomers. Our circle opened up and Theo and Opa filled in the space.

Just Theo and Opa.

"Where's Orion?" A sick feeling hit the pit of my stomach again, like reliving a nightmare. I hadn't seen him in a few hours. He left with Opa, but now Opa was right in front of me and Ri wasn't.

My heart started racing, my fingertips tickled. Holden slipped a grounding arm back around me, but I was too scared to look up and see my fear mirrored on his face.

"Oh," Opa looked a little abashed, "Madi and he are exploring the Farm." He stepped forward and patted my cheek, "I am sorry to scare you."

I felt a gust of air whoosh out of me, taking along with it most of my tension. I still didn't like not knowing exactly where he was, but I was certain Madi wouldn't let anything happen to him. I was more nervous for anyone who tried to do something.

Then, like I'd manifested them, Madi and Orion emerged from the trees at the edge of the Farm. Both were grinning wildly—and both looked a little wild. Their boots were covered in mud, and so were Madi's pants where Orion's shoes were resting as she held him. There were streaks on their faces, too, and pine needles stuck in their beanies and hair.

"I think it might be bath time," I heard Holden whisper in my ear. I nodded wide-eyed as they approached, nearness only increasing their bedraggled appearance.

"Baby," Theo stepped forward, looking increasingly more concerned. "What...What happened?" He gestured helplessly at the messy duo in front of us. And I found myself wondering the same thing.

"What?" She smiled innocently at him, "Nothing's broken."

He rolled his eyes, "And the mess?" When he glanced over at me, I caught his apologetic look.

"Manageable," she grunted as she handed Orion back over to me. His cheeks were flushed from the cold, and he looked so happy, I didn't care I'd end up covered in filth, too. "But we had fun, didn't we, Ri?" She tweaked his chin as he settled and he tucked up into my neck with another big smile.

"Found. Bun-nee," he clapped cheerfully in my arms. I looked up just in time to see Holden grinning down on him with more love than I could have ever hoped. *This is* definitely *what the Grinch felt like when his heart grew three sizes.*

"Yeah, we did!" Madi held up a hand for a high five and Orion giggled enthusiastically with his attempt to hit it.

Theo laughed, "C'mon, baby, let's get back to the Inn before you get the poor kid into any more trouble." His arm slipped over her shoulders and pulled her tight.

"Orion is *not* in trouble," I heard her pouting as he led her way. "He's so cute, though. *God.* Don't you want one?"

Theo froze and I felt Holden shake next to me. I looked up to see him attempting to smother what was sure to be a full howl of laughter. I shook my head and turned back toward the house. Ri wasn't in trouble, but he really did need that bath.

I heard Holden chasing after us, "Charlie said she was crazy. I think he may have been understating it a little bit."

"He loves her though," I smiled over my shoulder. Theo looked at Madi the way Holden looked at me. I was finally letting myself see it, too. And it was *everything*.

"Bet I love you more," he caught up to us and snuck his arms around my waist, lifting me, *holding Orion,* off the ground.

I squealed and kicked until he put us down. Orion thought

it was the greatest thing ever and kept chanting for him to do it again.

"You're obviously the crazy one in this relationship," I turned on Holden and he just grinned, quite satisfied I'd said the "R" word. I rolled my eyes, "But I love you, too."

Always had, always would.

HOLDEN

CHRISTMAS EVE BECAME a contender for my favorite day in the last five years. Unsurprisingly, all of my favorite days in the last five years had happened in the last few weeks. But we were making a new tradition on Christmas Eve: a Christmas sleepover in Oma's living room. Rosie, Orion, and me.

"All ready?" I yelled, toting Orion through my grandparent's house on my back, "Because we're coming!" I sprinted into the living room, spinning, and gently tossing the toddler onto the air mattress I was sure Rosie had just finished inflating.

"No," she laughed. One arm shot out to shove me, but I snagged her and twisted, dropping us both onto the couch. Rosie pinned to my chest.

Orion giggled maniacally as he struggled to make his way over to us.

"Get Auntie Ro," I told him causing Rosie to struggle more against me. "Get her, Ri. Tickle her."

Rosie squealed and tried to escape, but I wouldn't let go. *Never letting go.* Orion wasn't the most effective tickler in the world, but there was still time yet. He'd learn and then Rosie would really be in trouble. I couldn't wait.

"Okay, okay," Rosie panted a few minutes later and I finally loosed my hold just a little. Orion wasn't quite ready to give in, though, so Rosie sneaked an arm around him and pulled him in between us. She blew raspberries on his belly until he was squealing as loud as she'd been.

"Holden," Oma's voice carried into the living room, finally drawing an end to the giggle-fest, "There is someone here for you."

Rosie wriggled until she'd gotten both herself and Orion off of me. "Were you expecting someone?" I hated the way she still hesitated. The way she expected bad news to always come knocking. Although I really didn't know who was knocking, so I couldn't say much.

"No," I shook my head, then stood up and kissed her on the cheek, "But I'm sure it's nothing."

She followed me out of the living room toward the entry, Orion snugged into her chest protectively.

"Cute little hometown, Holden," Selby Hanover, a woman I hadn't seen since the day I turned in my packet stood shivering just inside Oma's front door, "Frazier said I could find you here."

I grinned at my friend. "It needs some work, but we'll bring it back to life." I slipped my arm around Rosie. I was sure the three of us made quite a picture. One I couldn't wait to hang on every single wall of our home. I'd put an offer in on a house in town, a house Rosie had always loved looking at growing up. I guessed the one good thing about everyone jumping ship was that her dream house was on the market.

It was going to be her Christmas gift. After five years, I wasn't fucking around. We knew where this was going. Where it had been leading all our lives. No need to slow the train now.

"Come in," Rosie extricated herself with a smile over her shoulder that told me she had some inkling about what I'd just been fantasizing about. Not the house. That was going to surprise the hell out of her. But the perfect picture. "I'm sure Oma's already got cocoa going."

"Thanks," she followed Rosie and I took up the rear on our way to the kitchen, "Sorry to drop in on you on Christmas Eve."

"Don't worry about it, Selby. Everything alright?" Not that I didn't appreciate a friend dropping in, but people didn't just show up places on Christmas Eve when things were going well.

She attempted a nonchalant shrug. I caught Rosie's eye and saw that she'd noticed it, too. "Just got out," Selby finally answered. "Thought I'd do some exploring. Visit some old friends."

Bullshit. But I wouldn't pry until she was ready. Might make Rosie try though. She was already pondering the woman who'd plopped down at the kitchen table looking far too weary for a casual visitor.

"You know," Selby continued before we could ask any more questions, "I meant what I said about this being a cute little town. I like the anonymity. I've been thinking about finding my own spot lately. Somewhere to settle down. Actually have a life, you know? Maybe start a business. I always thought I'd take over my parent's bakery before the market crashed and Uncle Sam came calling."

"Well," Rosie glanced over at me before shifting her attention back to Selby, "There's plenty of room for you here."

♠

ROSIE

One year later.

"Are you ready?" My sister's hands on my shoulder brought me back to the moment. To this room. A room I'd spent years playing and growing in. Where I had Christmas Eve slumber parties, and cried about losing my best friend.

I was still crying, but it wasn't because of a loss this time.

"Yeah," I nodded, and she carefully swept away the escaped tears. I had the baby months ago, but the hormonal weeping just wouldn't let up. Or maybe it was just me.

Lily's head bobbed and I watched her throat work as she fought her own tears. *Maybe it's just an Atwood thing.* "I'm so happy for you," she whispered, the sound barely escaping. "God, I'm a mess," she pulled away, her hand fluttering up around her face. I wasn't sure if she was trying to fan away tears or wave me off.

Either way, I laughed, too. It sounded just as watery as hers.

"Ugh," her groan was artificial and forced and made me laugh more, "We have to go before Holden thinks you've chickened out."

I let her tuck her arm into mine as she led me outside. The rush of cold air felt refreshing and soothing on my nerves. "Why would he? I wasn't the one who chickened out before."

Lily laughed next to me, rubbing her hands together, then up my arms sleeved in white. Clearly not as refreshed by the cold. Her wedding had been dead in the middle of summer. She also hadn't had to worry about fitting into her dress. But I couldn't begrudge her that. She made a wonderful mother to Daisy.

"Okay," she sighed and gave me one more once over before she found her seat, "Don't trip!"

"Wait, why would you—" I reached out for her arm but she

smiled at me and spun away, but not before she stuck her tongue out in an entirely un-Lily-like way. I couldn't do anything but laugh again as I made a much slower approach.

We decided to keep the wedding small. Just family and close friends in attendance. And all of the new Pinesbury. So not as small as we'd originally thought. But small towns were family, and we wanted our family.

But no wedding party. Because my best friend was the groom. And his was the bride. Butterflies swarmed in my stomach at the thought. *I get to marry my best friend.*

Standing alone at the end of the aisle, the distance between Holden and I felt like too much. But we'd come this far, gotten this close. There was no insurmountable distance between us anymore.

The music started and I took my first next steps toward the rest of our lives. Holden's eyes lit up, his signature grin tilting at the corners of his mouth. I barely contained a laugh, but it devolved into a short, but wracking sob. Holden chuckled back, then I lost his gaze as he brought his hand up to rub his nose. I squinted. *Hiding his own tears.*

I smiled this time.

It was perfect. Everything about this moment was everything I ever wanted. The Farm, the trees. The chill of a fresh snow giving me something else to blame for my pinkened nose.

Last year, I wasn't sure about anything. I wasn't sure how I could possibly raise a child, *grow* a child, or save an entire freaking Christmas tree farm. When Holden came back, I couldn't imagine how it would make anything better. Not when so much had happened, so much had gone wrong. I didn't know if there was any more Christmas magic left for me.

But, this Christmas, *I do.*

playlist

LETTERS FROM HOME - John Michael Montgomery
CHRISTMAS FEELS DIFFERENT THIS YEAR - Sarah Reeves
BACK HOME FOR CHRISTMAS - Mimi Webb
CHRISTMAS (BABY PLEASE COME HOME) - Mariah Carey
HOME - Cher, Michael Bublé
SANTA TELL ME - Arianna Grande
WANT TO - Sugarland
SNOWMAN - Sia
SNOWGLOBE - salem ilese
DRIVE BY - Train
CHRISTMAS TREE FARM - Taylor Swift
MISTLETOE - Ginuwine
BEING HERE, BEING THERE - Rod + Rose
UNDER THE TREE - Sam Palladio
MERRY CHRISTMAS - Ed Sheeran, Elton John
BONUS TRACK: **AFTER DECEMBER** - Brook Alexx

FIND THE **PINE FOR YOU** *PLAYLIST ON SPOTIFY!*

ANDERSON SECURITY SERIES

MISDIRECTION - Madi & Theo

Up Next:

MISCONCEPTION

Harper Vecellio has been playing a dangerous game. She's not morally bankrupt. But her life depends on everyone around her believing so. For years, she's defended the worst of the worst. Criminals willing to harm women, children, even their own families. But inside access gave her inside knowledge. Knowledge she leaked to the press to get her clients arrested and convicted. There was one person she trusted with the truth, and she let her down. Well, she didn't mean to. Not much the little journalist could do in the face of actual torture. But now Harper's on the run, and the last person she ever wanted to see again is here to help. And maybe fifteen years is a long time to hold a grudge. Especially against a high school nemesis. But it's not like the mob had ever been all that forgiving.

If there's one thing Max D'Amico never wanted, it was to ever set foot in Chicago again. At eighteen, he enlisted in the Marines and happily disappeared. He figured the one place they would never find him was in whatever hell-hole the US government dumped him in. And it worked. For fifteen years. But a post-separation career with Anderson Security brought him back to the Windy City, and with it came the secrets and danger he was desperate to escape. Now, he finds himself face-to-face with Chicago's biggest crime family: his own. And their latest target is the family's legal expert, Max's high school rival. Or that's what Harper thinks. She may protect what he's always hated, but Max has never once hated Harper Vecellio.

As Alpha Team finds themselves pulled in too many directions chasing a sadistic arms dealer, Harper and Max discover that while real family may have nothing to do with blood, the family they're born into will be deadly.

It's up to Max and Alpha Team to unearth secrets drowned in concrete.

Read Max and Harper's story, available Winter 2023-2024!

FAR FROM THE TRUTH

Isabella has always been isolated from the world of social media. On her sixteenth birthday, her strict mother allowed her to have the newest and hottest app, Honeybee. She was thrilled when she received a friend request from her best friend's brother, Elliott. Her secret crush. The two exchanged messages for months before Isabella felt something was off. She no longer believed it was Elliott she was talking to. Who could it be?

The teacher: Pays too much attention to his students

The cop: Makes everything his business

The lawyer: Objects to anyone being with her

What are their motives? Will she realize it in time?

acknowledgments

J.M. LEIGH

This one was a hard one for me sometimes. While we don't really love Rosie's sister right now, fertility issues are no easy challenge to face. And it's one I'm no stranger to. While these books are entirely fictional feats of imagination, the emotional experiences the characters go through come from a place of empathy. It was difficult to imagine what Rosie dealt with carrying her sister's child while I had no experience of that myself. I related more to our quasi-villian, Lily, the pain of *her* experience. What pain can turn into.

I'm so grateful to my friend and co-author, Alexis, for her support and insights on the matter. And for her love and support as a friend while I've experienced my own fertility challenges. It's not an easy topic, and it's deeply personal. But sometimes it falls into the taboo, and then it feels like a struggle you go through all alone. We shouldn't have to go it alone, though. I'm so appreciative of our friends and family who have been there for kind words of support, or as shoulders to cry on. This journey is so much easier to carry with their help.

And if you are facing the same struggles, I want you to know: YOU ARE NOT ALONE. We're here for you, Mama. One day at a time.

As always, I also owe an extra appreciative thank you to Mr. Leigh, my favorite cover artist and partner in life. He did not, fortunately, break his hand during the production of *this* cover. However, hands still posed a problem so we will be taking no criticism on them. *Thank you.* In all seriousness, though, we really challenged him with this one. He branched out in his aesthetic style and, one hundred percent, *understood the assignment.* (Are we still saying that?)

Finally, to the community I've built online, especially on Instagram and including my wonderful ARC Readers, you guys are *rock stars.* Seriously. I cannot express how much your support and kind words have meant to me. This has been a hell of a year, but you all made it so much better. I know I can count on you for the best book recommendations to distract me from all the stress and sadness, and even to swap stories and pep talks with. As is customary, I must say that sentimental messages are not my strong suit (and yes, we all know it's ironic that I somehow still write in the romance genre). But in this case, I don't think any sentimental turn of phrase would do the trick. The love and support you've shared has made a truly incalculable difference. You've added an extra spark in my life. One for which I will be eternally grateful.

From the bottom of my heart, *thank you.*

ALEXIS LAYNE

What a story! I am so grateful to be able to be writing a book with my best friend, a thought that had never crossed my mind! An idea that we both collaborated on and made it come true. Although this story does have a tough plot for some individuals, it's a great story. J.M. Leigh said it best, that you are NOT alone when it comes to fertility struggles.

Again, I am so happy and lucky to have a friend like J.M. Leigh. Collaborating on this story was so much fun. I am hoping that you readers love it as much as we did!

Thank you to my wonderful step-mom for reading the story and making sure there were no mistakes and supporting me in every decision and dream that I make.

Also, a huge thank you to those of you who followed along on social media and were excited about the release of this book!

Leigh loves a good mystery and characters you can fall in love with. Her stories tie together situational suspense, intense emotion, and a pinch of humor. Oh, and a splash of spice, too. They always have a happy ending, even while they still keep readers guessing about what will happen next.

www.jmleigh.com

facebook.com/authorjmleigh

x.com/authorjmleigh

instagram.com/authorjmleigh

tiktok.com/@j.m.leigh

amazon.com/J.M.-Leigh

bookbub.com/authors/j-m-leigh

goodreads.com/jmleigh

Alexis Layne loves to read romance, psychological thrillers, and a good mystery. She currently resides in Colorado with her husband and two beautiful kids.

instagram.com/authoralexislayne

www.ingramcontent.com/pod-product-compliance
Lightning Source LLC
Chambersburg PA
CBHW032014170626
46807CB00006B/2807